NOTES FROM THE ██████ LIFE OF A TOTAL GENIUS

by Stacey Matson

illustrations by Simon Kwan

Scholastic Canada Ltd.

Toronto New York London Auckland Sydney
Mexico City New Delhi Hong Kong Buenos Aires

Scholastic Canada Ltd.
604 King Street West, Toronto, Ontario M5V 1E1, Canada

Scholastic Inc.
557 Broadway, New York, NY 10012, USA

Scholastic Australia Pty Limited
PO Box 579, Gosford, NSW 2250, Australia

Scholastic New Zealand Limited
Private Bag 94407, Botany, Manukau 2163, New Zealand

Scholastic Children's Books
Euston House, 24 Eversholt Street, London NW1 1DB, UK

www.scholastic.ca

Library and Archives Canada Cataloguing in Publication

Matson, Stacey, author
        Notes from the [text blacked out] life of a total genius
/ Stacey Matson ; illustrations by Simon Kwan.

In the title the word before "life" is blacked out and illegible.
Issued in print and electronic formats.
Notes from the [text blacked out] life of a total genius.
ISBN 978-1-4431-4823-8 (hardback).--ISBN 978-1-4431-4824-5
(paperback).--ISBN 978-1-4431-4825-2 (html)

        I. Kwan, Simon (Illustrator), illustrator II. Title.
III. Title: Notes from the life of a total genius.

PS8626.A839N68 2016   jC813'.6   C2016-900932-7

Cover images: Boy, © IkazNarsis/Shutterstock, Inc.; Censored, ©
Thomas Pajot/Shutterstock, Inc.

6 5 4 3 2 1   Printed in Canada 114   16 17 18 19 20 21

For Curtiss,
whose email style I can only try to emulate;
and for Chelsey,
who instilled in me the daily need for both
dark green and orange vegetables.

SEPTEMBER

testing . . . texting . . .

Who is this?

its rob

Who?

rob zack moron. this is my new #

Robbie! How's it going man? How's Lethbridge? What's your new school like?

ok I guess. girls r hot. im gonna go 4 football

I wish you were here. This week has been so weird without you!

New teachers this year too (none are hot). I have Ms Whitehead again for English.

Three years running. Clearly she can't get enough of the Bean! Ha!

> I'll send you an email about it all. Too much to write in a text.

> ya i can tell.

From: Arthur Bean (arthuraaronbean@gmail.com)
To: Robbie Zack (robbiethegreat2000@hotmail.com)
Sent: September 4, 19:42

Dear Robbie,

All right, so first, they painted the cafeteria. It's still white, but they want to put a big mural on one wall. If you were here, you could have entered the contest to design it. That would have been awesome. Other than that, everything is pretty much the same at school as last year. Except for the new teachers, like I mentioned. The new principal is Ms Kraleigh. No word on what she's like yet. I'm taking Drama this year too, so I met the new Drama teacher. His name is Mr. Harker, but he said that he hates being called Mister. So instead we are going to call him Hark. I asked him if he was an angel (like the Christmas carol) and if he could sing, and he said that he can but once he gets going, he can't stop singing and that he wouldn't torture us with his extensive musical knowledge. He's really cool. If you were here, you would like him. He's funny and he wants us to do cool stuff and really push the envelope this year.

Other than that, things are pretty normal here. I have my first meeting with Mr. Everett about Kennedy and me being co-editors of the newspaper.

I haven't talked to Kennedy at all this week. I saw her in English, Science and French, and yesterday at lunch, and I saw her today between classes but I barely noticed her at all. She looked really tanned. I don't know where she went for summer vacation. Probably somewhere fancy. She still hangs out with Catie too, but I don't know why anyone would choose to hang out with Catie. Girls remain a mystery.

How was the last week of camp? I'm sorry I had to leave before we finished our film. Did it turn out all right? Camping with my dad was OK. We were right beside a lake, but it was freezing, not like at Flying Spirit camp. I can't believe I had to leave one camp to go camp somewhere else! Hanging with my dad got a bit boring too, so I was glad that Luke came with us. It's too bad you couldn't come. Maybe you and Luke will visit at the same time this year and you guys can meet. Clearly, your mom didn't plan moving away properly. My cousin lives in Edmonton. You live in the exact opposite direction. Did she not think about me at all in her relocation?

Ha! Just kidding.

Sorry. I just realized that this is really long. I hope you actually read the whole thing.

Yours truly,
Arthur Bean

From: Robbie Zack (robbiethegreat2000@hotmail.com)
To: Arthur Bean (arthuraaronbean@gmail.com)
Sent: September 4, 22:00

hey artie

ya things here r weird. living w mom again means that shes allways around and makes me lunch to take. like i want to bring a lunch! i told her i can eat at the caf, but she says its unhealthy. caleb stays in his room all day and theres alot of yelling.

so far my new school sux. its really small and no one talks to me. witch is kind of like the end of last yr in Calgary anyway. Ha! im allready planning coming home.

rz

▸▸ ▸▸ ▸▸

September 5th

Dear RJ,

It seems so strange to be in grade nine. It feels like just yesterday that I was afraid of the grade nines. They were so much cooler than us! Now there are kids in the lower grades who will worship me! Ha! Hopefully all the adoration won't go to my head.

First things first, I need to convince Robbie to move back to Calgary. I still can't believe he would choose to live in Lethbridge with his mom. So far, grade nine sucks without him here.

I didn't have anyone to eat lunch with, so I ate by my locker and felt like a nerd. I hate feeling like a nerd. Until I can either get new friends or convince Robbie to move home, it looks like it's just me and you, my trusty RJ. A reading journal as a friend . . . man, I AM a nerd.

I have big plans for tomorrow though. I'm going to find out if Kennedy is talking to me. She's probably figured out by now that all the stuff people said about Robbie last year was made up. And then she will apologize for everything that happened last year, and we can hang out again. By hang out, I mean as *friends*. I don't even want to date her anymore. I'm a cool, single guy at the top of the school chain. Let the ladies line up! Kennedy will see exactly what she missed out on!

Yours truly,
Arthur Bean

▶▶ ▶▶ ▶▶

Assignment: Goals for the Year

Welcome back, grade nines! I'm glad to see some familiar faces in my class, and to see some new ones, too. I'm certain we're going to have a great final year together. This year's English curriculum focuses on strengthening your writing and critical thinking skills. We'll be exploring new literary devices and opening our minds to different writing genres in fun, creative ways.

In order to get more out of this year, take some time to reflect on what you would like to work on. Maybe you'd like to be a greater grammarian. Perhaps you want to polish up your poetry prowess, or strengthen your summarizing skills. It's important to set some personal goals, since each of you has your own strengths and challenges. Think about what you want to accomplish in your final year of junior high English. Come up with three well-defined goals for yourself, and write them down. Let's see if we can meet these goals together!

Due: September 10

Hey, Artie! Hey, Kennedy!

I'm excited to be working with two very fine reporters this year as the Terry Fox Jr. High Marathon editors. You're both extremely strong writers, and you have complementary skills to bring depth to the school newspaper this year. So, before we go on, thank you for taking on this challenge. It's not going to be easy, but we'll work together as a team to make the Marathon the best it can be! Remember, though: there's no "i" in team, but there is one in "deadline."

I know you two are friends, which is good, because you can run ideas past each other between meetings. We'll spend the next meeting brainstorming some great ideas for stories, and marking key events on the Marathon calendar so that we're ready to send our reporters out on the scene. Let me know if you have any questions or concerns before we start. Otherwise, let's make this year great by being concise, clear and objective! We'll be the only paper that is black, white, read all over and totally transparent!

Cheers!
Mr. E.

Dear Mr. Everett,

First, I'd like to thank you for the opportunity to run the newspaper. As you know, I've been working hard to hone my unique editorial voice over the last couple of years, and I'm definitely ready to let it be heard. I expect that Kennedy and I are on the same page, or at least in the same newspaper section, when it comes to the direction of the Marathon this year. I, for one, would like to get rid of the sports page because I'm pretty sure no one reads it. After all, it's only there for the kids who are on sports teams, and I don't think they ever read anything. I think we should have a bigger editorial section and also write about important national and municipal issues. We could use my assignments from Social Studies for this part, since Ms Denault is making us watch the news and respond to it. In fact, if we publish my assignments, it might make my homework better. I definitely write my best work when I know there will be a big audience.

These are just a few of my ideas. Obviously, there will be more.

Yours truly,
Arthur Bean

Artie,

Hmm, maybe I needed to be clearer: You're not, as you put it, "running the paper." As a co-editor you, Kennedy and I will be working <u>together</u> to plan out the paper each week. There will be some editorial articles, but I want you to remember the numerous conversations we've had over the past two years about being kind and being objective. Don't rush to conclusions about other students; remarks like your assumption that athletic students don't read are exactly what need to be avoided. As a side note, I can't tell if you're joking about publishing your homework; if you were, that's a good one, since it's clearly never going to happen!

I really do appreciate that you have big ideas for the paper, and we can talk about all of them. I'm as stoked as you are about this year, and you're a great writer and a radical dude. But it's going to be important to be aware of other people even more this year. As you young kids say, check yourself before you wreck yourself!

Cheers!
Mr. E.

▶▶ ▶▶ ▶▶

From: Robbie Zack (robbiethegreat2000@hotmail.com)
To: Arthur Bean (arthuraaronbean@gmail.com)
Sent: September 7, 11:45

i was bored last nite so i did a thing 4 ur paper.

From: Arthur Bean (arthuraaronbean@gmail.com)
To: Robbie Zack (robbiethegreat2000@hotmail.com)
Sent: September 7, 13:08

Dear Robbie,

That's awesome! Maybe we can use it for the masthead, although I probably have to ask Kennedy and Mr. Everett. I talked to Kennedy at our editors meeting on Friday. I know you don't care, and neither do I, but she said that she went to BC with Catie's family for part of the summer. We kind of talked a bit about non-newspaper stuff. It was pretty normal, almost like nothing happened last year between her and me. I don't know if she's still dating the same guy. I didn't ask, because it doesn't matter to me at all. I'm so over her. It's almost scary how much I don't care. I mean, I still think she's nice, but just in a friend way. Anyway, it doesn't matter.

Yours truly,
Arthur Bean

▶▶ ▶▶ ▶▶

To Ms Whitehead,

This is a contract between Arthur Bean and himself regarding his English class. This year his goals in grade nine English are the following. If he doesn't reach them, the punishment is most certainly death (or maybe an F).

1. I will finish writing a novel. My novel has to be at least 100,000 words long.

2. I will write every assignment I can in verse to practise my rhyming techniques.

3. I will hand in every assignment on time, and they will all have my name on them.

I think that these three goals speak to my strengths and weaknesses.

Signed by,
Arthur Bean

and notarized by
Arthur Bean

Arthur,

I'm glad to see you in my class again and I look forward to your unique take on assignments. You're a strong writer, and I've enjoyed watching you discover new abilities in your own writing. However, this first assignment is meant to help guide your studies for the year. Your first goal is drastically unrealistic. I'm happy to assist you in writing a novel this year, but most of that writing will be done on your own time, and homework assignments need to take precedence. Your second goal is also unreasonable; there will be some assignments where you can choose your format, but writing everything in rhyme doesn't help you to develop other writing skills. Your third goal is fine, if not a little underwhelming. I know we discussed punctuality last year, but I don't believe that handing work in on time really pushes you to challenge yourself in new ways. It's expected that your homework will be on time anyway. Please, either re-send me your goals, or see me after class and we can form some goals together that are more realistic.

Ms Whitehead

Dear Ms Whitehead,

Here are my amended goals:

1. My assignments will be longer than everyone else's;

2. I will read at least one non-fiction book (and tell you about it);

3. I will learn the proper use of a semi-colon and use it in every assignment at least once. (See how I'm already succeeding in this last goal?) (See how my punctuality is right on time?)

And as a bonus goal,

4. I will make sure that all my assignments are based on true stories.

From: Arthur Bean (arthuraaronbean@gmail.com)
To: Kennedy Laurel (imsocutekl@hotmail.com)
Sent: September 10, 19:03

Dear Kennedy,

I just thought I should say that I'm thinking about developing a running opinion column for the *Marathon*. It would be super great if you wanted to hang out after school or on the weekend and help me come up with some awesome ideas of things I could write about. I want to focus on big issues that affect everyone. I know you and I work well together, so we could have a great brainstorming session.

What do you think?

Yours truly,
Arthur Bean

From: Kennedy Laurel (imsocutekl@hotmail.com)
To: Arthur Bean (arthuraaronbean@gmail.com)
Sent: September 10, 21:57

Hi Arthur!

Your column sounds like a great idea! I'm REALLY busy though, so I can't meet! I'm on like a THOUSAND committees and stuff this year, plus I want to make sure I have time to see my friends and my boyfriend too!

Actually, maybe you can help me out! Do you think you'd be able to work the bake-sale booth for the fall carnival next week?! That would be AMAZING! I would be SOOO appreciative! It's only a few hours after school on the 13th (SO UNLUCKY LOL!) and you can ask any of your friends to help out! ALL my friends are running booths! I feel bad asking, but you're my last shot LOL!

Kennedy ☺

From: Arthur Bean (arthuraaronbean@gmail.com)
To: Kennedy Laurel (imsocutekl@hotmail.com)
Sent: September 10, 22:10

Dear Kennedy,

I could probably run the booth for you. That's what friends are for, right? Plus, then you'll owe me a favour! Haha!

Yours truly,
Arthur Bean

▶▶ ▶▶ ▶▶

September 11th

Dear RJ,

I think Robbie's lonely in Lethbridge, so I've been writing him. I try and tell him about the crappy stuff at school so that he doesn't get too sad about not being here. Not that he had a great time last year. I even heard some kids talking about how he isn't at school this year because he's in juvie. Kids are so stupid sometimes. I vow, RJ, I'm never going to believe rumours!

I've been trying to make a bunch of new friends too. Kennedy is friends with practically everyone, so I think that she'll invite me to parties and stuff. Right now, though, I've been eating lunch alone at my locker. At least my locker is over by the Home Ec room, and no one goes there during lunch, so I don't look like a total loser. Well, Von saw me one day and told me I could sit with him, but that guy is so, so (I've written *so* twice to show my supreme annoyance) annoying. Why does he think he's so amazing at everything? And more importantly, why does he tell everyone? I told him that I'm working on my novel over lunch. At first I was going to tell him I was writing a movie, but he would have forced his way into "helping" like last year, and that went terribly. I'm getting smarter in my old age, RJ.

The rest of school is all right. I've got pretty good teachers this year, none of the really hard or mean ones. Actually, Mr. Everett is a hard marker, but he's so dorky and happy all the time that it's kind of OK. I really like Hark, the new Drama teacher. He's seriously awesome. I can't even say why, but it's like he isn't trying too hard. So many teachers try so hard to get you to like them and it's very transparent and that makes me like them less. But Hark doesn't do that. He's kind of awkward in front of us, but he knows so much about theatre. He said that we're going to start by performing poems by famous people. And I know that sounds really stupid, but we're allowed to do any poem we want. Like, anything! If Robbie were in the class, I bet he'd do a Dr. Seuss poem or something like that just to see if Hark meant "anything." I don't know what I'm going to do. Maybe I'll write my own poem. I can do it at lunch. There's nothing else to do!

Yours truly,
Arthur Bean

▶▶　▶▶　▶▶

People were asking about you at school today. They totally miss you.

i think ur phone auto-correctted on u. u meant that they diss me.

No, I didn't.

You didn't miss anything today. Lunch sucked. Pasta primavera.

better than salad that my mom sent. everyday she sends me w/ salad. i think she thinks im a bunny

Can't really picture you as Robbie Rabbit.

Awwwww . . . Aren't you a cute bunny?!?!

ive got football triouts 2morro.

Good luck! You'll get in for sure. You dominated capture the flag at camp this summer.

Ya, I OWNED that flag man. will keep u posted.

From: Von Ipo (thenexteastwood@hotmail.com)
To: Arthur Bean (arthuraaronbean@gmail.com)
Sent: September 12, 19:56

Hey, Artie!

First, don't you love Hark? That guy is awesome! Do you have a poem yet for Drama? If you need one, I've chosen twenty! I basically went through my shelves and picked the best ones, but I can only do one. I chose a Walt Whitman poem, but I'm going to ask if I can do a Jay Z rap as a poem. Rap is basically poetry. Maybe Hark'll even let me play the real song in the background. Let me know if you want to look through what I have. Some people are doing their performances in partners. Be cool if we did something together, hey? Like our movie last year! Let me know!

Cheers!
Von

▶▶ ▶▶ ▶▶

Assignment: Personal Reading Projects

Although we will be doing a novel study this year in class, as well as studying one of Shakespeare's tragedies (here's a hint for you: Double, double, toil and trouble . . .), there will also be some individual reading and responses. Over the course of the year, you are expected to read and review at least one of the novels on the approved reading list, one biography or autobiography and one non-fiction book. Of course, you're welcome to read and respond to more books if you wish! If there is a specific book that you wish to review that is not on the list, please speak to me. You must log your responses through detailed book reviews. I expect more than a synopsis! Chart your progress and reflections as you read.

There is no specific due date, but I suggest you plan your year accordingly, so that you aren't handing them all in at the end of June. Book reviews submitted after June 3 will be marked as late.

▶▶ ▶▶ ▶▶

From: Kennedy Laurel (imsocutekl@hotmail.com)
To: Arthur Bean (arthuraaronbean@gmail.com)
Sent: September 14, 11:16

Hi Arthur!

Thanks SO much for running the bake-sale booth!
Wasn't the carnival super fun?? It was HILARIOUS
to see Catie in the dunk tank! She was so mouthy,
I'm not surprised that she got dunked so often
LOL! I'm going to write an article for the *Marathon*
about how it brought together the school in such a
positive way!

   Anyway, I just wanted to talk to you about
something. Someone saw you eat a Rice Krispie
square while you were sitting there, but they didn't
see you pay for it! I'm sure it's just a mix-up, but I
promised that I would follow up!

Kennedy ☺

From: Arthur Bean (arthuraaronbean@gmail.com)
To: Kennedy Laurel (imsocutekl@hotmail.com)
Sent: September 14, 14:41

Dear Kennedy,

I'm glad that the carnival went pretty well. I didn't
really get a chance to see any of it, since I was the
only person working my booth the whole time. And
your "secret source" is right. I did eat the last Rice
Krispie square without paying for it. I never got a
chance to eat dinner, and it was the last one and the

carnival had already closed, so I didn't think it was a big deal. I was so hungry! I didn't know that you had spies watching! You must know EVERYTHING that happens in the school hahaha!

Did you want me to pay for the Rice Krispie square? Do you want help writing your article?

Yours truly,
Arthur Bean

From: Kennedy Laurel (imsocutekl@hotmail.com)
To: Arthur Bean (arthuraaronbean@gmail.com)
Sent: September 14, 16:20

Hi Arthur!

OF COURSE NOT! You don't have to pay for it! I just wanted to check up!

I DO have spies everywhere! So you better watch your step LOL! One false move, and you're OFF the friend list LOL!

I already wrote the article today! I wanted to get it done because Jerry's having an awesome birthday party tonight! It's Disney themed LOL! Can't wait to go!!

Kennedy ☺

▸▸ ▸▸ ▸▸

From: Arthur Bean (arthuraaronbean@gmail.com)
To: Robbie Zack (robbiethegreat2000@hotmail.com)
Sent: September 17, 11:43

Dear Robbie,

How did the football tryouts go? When will you find out? I still can't believe you want to be on the football team. I thought you were going to focus on art this year! Speaking of which, I can get you a spot doing a comic strip for the *Marathon*. I called it "The Out of Towners" so that you can draw it, but no one will know it was you. It will be brilliant. I can tell you all the gossip around the school and then you can make fun of it in your comic.

This week we got a ton of Math homework. I'm going to be doing it all weekend. But the new Drama teacher, Hark, started a playwright club AND it's only open to grade nines and a few grade eights. It's really serious. We're going to put on our own plays this year! If you were here, we could have totally made Zombie School into a play (it would be better as a play than Von's dumb movie anyway), but I don't want to "steal your ideas" (as you like to remind me), so I'm going to do something else. I really thought Kennedy was going to join the group too, but she didn't. Not that I care, I just thought it was weird. It's probably for the best. I don't really want to have to see her all the time anyway. She's being so bossy at the newspaper meetings. It's like she thinks she has the final say on everything.

Are you coming back to spend Thanksgiving with your dad? I hope so.

Yours truly,
Arthur Bean

From: Robbie Zack (robbiethegreat2000@hotmail.com)
To: Arthur Bean (arthuraaronbean@gmail.com)
Sent: September 17, 15:04

i find out about the team next week, but i think i made it!

playrites sounds cool. my acting career ended with romeo and juliett. i was a child star whose star faded. HA! besides, my school is putting on a musicall and i am def NOT a singer.

i def dont want to do ur comic strip. if i do any art, it wont be as boring as that sounds. im going to be an art and football star. watch out marshawn lynch! im more talented than u! HA!

im back a round thanksgiving. see u then 4 sure.

Rob

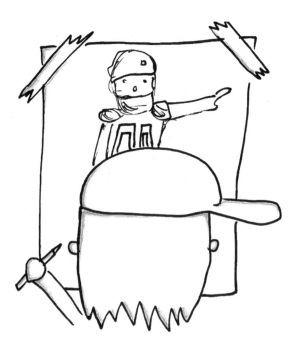

⏩ ⏩ ⏩

Dear Hark,

Here's my poem for the performance poetry assignment. What do you think? I wanted to go with something classic at first, but I didn't know what to do and it all sounded so boring. I thought about using a Jay Z rap song, but Von told me he was doing that. Instead I wrote this over the weekend. Is it OK? I don't want to sound stupid, especially if everyone else is doing a famous poem and mine is the only one that isn't famous. Maybe it's not even all that good. I bet you'll be honest with me. You seem like the type of guy who would be honest with his students. Anyway, I made sure it didn't rhyme because I didn't want it to sound too childish and I looked through all your poetry books and just used their style of free verse.

Yours truly,
Arthur Bean

I'm No Detective

By Arthur Bean

I'm no detective,
but
I can't help but notice that you're around.
Maybe it's by accident
That you're close by
That your seat is next to mine
More than it isn't next to mine
It could just be a coincidence
That I saw you near my house
In the rain
In the nighttime
Under an umbrella
Under a tree
Looking around
Looking lost
It could be a lucky shot
That you were at the restaurant that night
We all know the pizza coupons
Are only good on Thursdays
So of course everyone is there
Everyone who is anyone is there
But maybe
These are clues to something more
Something exciting
Something true
But who am I to say?
I'm no detective.

Hi, Arthur!

First off, I love your poem. It's fantastic! It's mysterious and a little creepy, in a really good way. It's hard to say if your narrator is telling the truth or not. Is he the stalker, or is he being stalked? This is great work. Has anyone ever told you you're a great writer? This is going to be just perfect; we'll work on staging it in a way that adds to the mystery of the piece on Thursday in class. This year is going to be great, isn't it? I really appreciate getting your reflection on the piece too. Let's keep that up! I like knowing what you're thinking about when you're writing. It helps me to understand your intention and help you achieve what you want.

I'm so pleased to have a gang of students who are serious about theatre. This is what teaching is all about. You guys inspire me, you really do!

Hark

▶▶ ▶▶ ▶▶

Assignment: Reviewing Personification

Imbuing non-living objects with human-like characteristics adds effect and a unique voice to your work. This is called personification, and can be an excellent descriptive technique. Create ten sentences personifying objects you find in your house.

Due: September 23

▶▶ ▶▶ ▶▶

Personification Sentences

By Arthur Bean

1. The ice cream in the freezer was calling my name. It cried out in despair, "Eat me, Arthur! Eat me!"
2. The computer stared back at me, blankly.
3. The books on my bookcase squeezed into line to make room for one more.
4. The blanket was snuggled deep into the couch cushions.
5. Even the kitchen held its nose at the smell coming off the garbage can.
6. The kitty litter box begged to be emptied.
7. The lemon puckered its lips in distaste.
8. The corn perked up its ears at the sound of the water boiling.
9. The potato eyed the tinfoil, knowing that it spelled the end of the potato's life.
10. The cherry felt sad in the pit of his stomach.

Arthur,

You started off very strong, but the last three examples descend into puns rather than personification. You have a keen sense of description, and I'd like to see you challenge yourself this year to use different literary devices to bring your work to a higher level.

Ms Whitehead

From: Kennedy Laurel (imsocutekl@hotmail.com)
To: Arthur Bean (arthuraaronbean@gmail.com)
Sent: September 23, 19:50

Hi Arthur!

I was looking over the list of "hot topics" that you brought to the *Marathon* meeting and I want the student body (as much as I HATE that term ☺) to feel like it's really about them. I LOVE your idea of having a creative corner where students can submit their own work in the paper to share it, but do you think they would go for it? Most kids aren't going to do more writing OUTSIDE of class than they have to.

   It's really about making this the best year ever for the *Marathon*! And it's so important to me because, don't tell anyone, but I'm trying to win the school leadership award! They only give one out if there's a student who REALLY deserves it! So I'm working like Supergirl to win it! It means a lot to me to be recognized as a leader, which sounds SO lame to say, but it's true! It's so much work though! I feel like I need to make clones of myself to do all the things I've signed up for LOL!

   I guess what I want to get across is that the *Marathon* is a REALLY big part of my plan to win!

Kennedy ☺

From: Arthur Bean (arthuraaronbean@gmail.com)
To: Kennedy Laurel (imsocutekl@hotmail.com)
Sent: September 23, 21:43

Dear Kennedy,

I didn't even know there was a leadership award. I think you'd be a great choice for it! I'm happy to help you out on anything that you need. That's what friends are for, right? Do you want to hang out after school sometime this week? I can help you plan your strategy, and then we can catch up with other people. I can never keep track of stuff happening, I'm invited to so many things!

Yours truly,
Arthur Bean

From: Kennedy Laurel (imsocutekl@hotmail.com)
To: Arthur Bean (arthuraaronbean@gmail.com)
Sent: September 23, 22:02

Hi Arthur!

I can't meet tomorrow. I'm campaigning for the grad committee (no surprise there, hey? LOL). I want our grad to be THE BEST, so Catie and I have been working really hard to make posters to get everyone excited for the end of the year (I KNOW! A LITTLE early LOL!). Plus, it might be a bit weird, just you and me. I mean, we are TOTALLY friends, but I don't know if we're friends who hang out. That might be weird! Right now, everything is so OK between us. I don't want to ruin that!

Kennedy ☺

From: Arthur Bean (arthuraaronbean@gmail.com)
To: Kennedy Laurel (imsocutekl@hotmail.com)
Sent: September 23, 22:40

Dear Kennedy,

Of course. That totally makes sense. I'm cool with that. Cool as a cucumber!

Yours truly,
Arthur Bean

▶▶ ▶▶ ▶▶

> This new playwriting group is awesome! I wish you could be in it. We decided to call ourselves The Leg Breakers. Get it?

like the moffia?

> Sure, like the mafia.

> It's a play on words. Like Break a Leg.

PLAY on words?!?! hahaha

> That's not what I mean.

i know

Maybe you can be in it from Lethbridge! I can ask Hark. You could submit stuff by email or you can Skype in!

Then you & I could write together! It would be awesome. I do my best work when you're here. I was thinking of writing a play about time-travelling aliens who save Earth!

do u mean u do MY best work when im there hahaha

Are you ever going to let that go?

nope hahaha

▶▶ ▶▶ ▶▶

Arthur, Editor: Meet the Creatures

By Arthur Bean

There are plenty of new student faces around this year, but also a few new teachers. I had the opportunity to speak to the three new teachers at Terry Fox Jr. High, and find out a little more about them to share with you, my readers.

I first talked to Mr. Harker. Mr. Harker's full name is Hector Harker, which he said "makes him feel like a character in a bad children's book." He has always hated his name, and he thinks that's one of the reasons he went into theatre. He said that "he could play a character with any other name than his own."

He went to the National Theatre School in Montreal, and after that, he was in a touring production of *Cats* for a couple of years. When he got tired of dressing as a feline, he moved to Toronto, where he did a couple of plays and was an extra in some movies, including a movie starring Robin Williams, but he never met him in person. He was also in the chorus of *Wicked,* which is another musical, for two months, before he quit and went back to school to become a teacher. Mr. Harker moved to Calgary last year, and he said that he's super stoked to be at such an amazing school with such great kids. He said that he plans to do a student-written play festival this spring, and that he is here to learn as much from his students as he hopes they learn from him. With such a wealth of practical theatre and film experience, and his awesome ideas for theatre in our school, I can say with full certainty that we're lucky to have him here!

Ms Kraleigh is the new principal. She used to work at a high school in the southwest. She is married, and before she became a principal, I think she taught Chemistry.

There is also Mrs. Lahiri. She's the new grade seven Math teacher. This is her first year teaching (you know what that means!).

If you see Mr. Harker, or any of the other new teachers in the hallways, be sure to say hello. It's always a good idea to stay on their good side!

Hi, Arthur!

You did a great job interviewing Mr. Harker. He's a cool guy; I've been chatting with him during lunch too and he's got a great sense of humour, much like myself! I think, though, that

Ms Kraleigh and Mrs. Lahiri didn't get a fair shot here. Here are your choices as Editor: you can cut down the interview with Mr. Harker and add more to the profiles of the other two teachers, or you can keep the interview with Mr. Harker and have equally in-depth interviews with Ms Kraleigh and Mrs. Lahiri in the next editions. Mrs. Lahiri's interview could focus on her use of fractions; I hear she's partial to them. Or maybe, because she's the Math teacher, she has a lot of problems! I do know that her class on the use of decimals definitely has a point!

Cheers!
Mr. E.

Dear Mr. Everett,

I guess I could do that. I'll set up time with the principal to meet her. Maybe people will see me going into her office and think I'm a badass!

Yours truly,
Arthur Bean

▶▶ ▶▶ ▶▶

From: Von Ipo (thenexteastwood@hotmail.com)
To: Arthur Bean (arthuraaronbean@gmail.com)
Sent: September 27, 11:20

Hey Artie!

Loved your poem for Drama. It was awesome! It reminded
me of this poem I wrote once that was about a detective
and the guy he was chasing. It was a lot longer than
your poem though. Literally thirteen pages long! Was
awesome though. They were going to publish it in the
Globe and Mail, but it was too long. Anyway, do you want
to be partners for the dialogue work this week? It would
be awesome to work with you, and we did so awesome
last year. Plus, I think you and I are basically the best
writers in the group. You come up with amazing ideas.
    What do you think? Let me know!

Von

From: Arthur Bean (arthuraaronbean@gmail.com)
To: Von Ipo (thenexteastwood@hotmail.com)
Sent: September 27, 13:07

Von,

Hark said that he was pairing us up, so I'm sure that
he has better judgment about who should be writing
with whom. So if we get paired up, then we have to
work together, OK?

Arthur Bean

From: Von Ipo (thenexteastwood@hotmail.com)
To: Arthur Bean (arthuraaronbean@gmail.com)
Sent: September 27, 13:10

Oh yeah, I asked him already if we could be partners and he said that he thought that was a great idea! He's awesome, eh? Love that guy!

Von

Assignment: Onomatopoeia Comics

Using some of your favourite onomatopoeic words, create a short comic strip.

It can be about anything you want, but you must use onomatopoeic words as both sounds and dialogue.

Due: October 2

▸▸ ▸▸ ▸▸

September 28th

Dear RJ,

This has been the most boring weekend ever. I wanted to call someone to hang out, but then there was no one to call. Luke is in Edmonton, plus I don't know if cousins count as friends. Robbie's in Lethbridge and he doesn't really have a lot to say anyway. I called him, but after five minutes, I could tell he was just watching TV, so I told him I had to go. I thought about calling Kennedy, but I didn't want to push our friendship. I need to wait a bit so that I don't seem super desperate to hang out. She still acts a bit strange and nervous when I'm around, like she thinks I'm going to ask her on a date. Which, RJ, I'm not going to do. I learned my lesson last year. If she wants to date me, she has to ask *me* this time. But until then, I can't ask her to hang out on the weekend. So then I spent an hour scrolling through the contacts in my phone, looking for people to call. I couldn't find anyone! Oliver and I used to hang out in elementary school, but he's really into sports and I'm not. So that leaves Von, who I can't handle, and my dad. Any suggestions, RJ? I don't think I'm a bad guy. I'm pretty interesting. I'm funny. I can do a really good impression of Mrs. Ireland. So how do I make new friends at school when everyone already knows me AND has their own gang?

I guess I'll go back to my book.

Yours truly,
Arthur Bean

OCTOBER

Arthur,

I'm pleased to see your unique choice of words! I hope you had fun discovering onomatopoeic words and integrating many different sounds into your comic.

Ms Whitehead

Ms Whitehead,

It was really easy. I just Googled words and found a billion of them. Maybe even a google of them. You should make the assignments more challenging if you want us to perform at a grade nine level. So far, this year is a breeze!

Yours truly,
Arthur Bean

▶▶ ▶▶ ▶▶

Dear Hark,

Here's the dialogue assignment from me and Von. It's not my best work. I don't think that we were able to find a rhythm together, like you wanted us to. We also got assigned a really weird setting. I'm not blaming you, but next time maybe I should work alone. Or else, maybe I could work with Ben Crisp. He's a funny guy; I bet we could come up with some amazing stuff. Anyway, please don't judge me too harshly!

Yours truly,
Arthur Bean

Dialogue Assignment: Arthur and Von

Setting: Inside a Cookie Factory

Georgina: If I see another cream-filled chocolate chip cookie, I will kill myself.

Jennifer: Haha! I know!

Georgina: It's not funny. I will throw myself under the cookie press and end it all.

Jennifer: Me too!

Georgina: All these cookies go past, and every day, all I get to do is press a button to add the vanilla cream. Every 10 seconds, I press the same button. 10 . . . 9 . . . 8 . . . 7 . . . 6 . . . 5 . . . 4 . . . 3 . . . 2 . . . 1 . . . cream . . . 10 . . . It's not worth living for.

Jennifer: I do that too!

Georgina: You do what, Jennifer? Repeat everything I say? Follow me around like a lost puppy? Are you in love with me, Jennifer?

Jennifer: Haha! No!

Georgina: Then why do you do these things, Jennifer? Are you trying to become me, Jennifer?!

Jennifer: No!

Georgina: I think you are, Jennifer. In fact, I noticed that you bought the same frosted pink lipstick that I own. And you've started wearing your hair the same as me inside your hairnet. That was my signature style, Jennifer. What else have you done?

Jennifer: Nothing!

Georgina: Now that I'm actually looking at you, I think you've had a nose job, haven't you? You're literally trying to become me!

Jennifer: What are you talking about?

Georgina: Don't play dumb with me, Jennifer. I've seen you sneaking photos of me while I've been working. I've watched you practising my perfect model walk during our ten-minute lunch hour. And I saw you talking to my husband the other day. I won't stand for it, Jennifer!

Jennifer: I was asking your husband for directions to the bus stop.

Georgina: Oh, SURE you were! You know, Jennifer, you'll never be good enough to press the cream button. I know you think you can do it. Sure, it looks like the flour button, or the butter-adding button, but there's an art to this button. I've worked here for 56 years to get to the cream button and there's no way that I'm giving it up before I die. Especially not to an idiotic moron like yourself!

Jennifer: I don't think you can use the words idiotic or moron.

Georgina: Can't I, Jennifer? What else can't I do? Can I not . . . pull off your hairnet? (She pulls off Jennifer's hairnet.)

Jennifer: What are you doing?!

Georgina: Can I not . . . rip the sleeves off your uniform? (She rips off the sleeves of Jennifer's uniform.)

Jennifer: Stop it!

Georgina: Can I not . . . get rid of you forever?!?! (She pushes Jennifer into the cookie press.)

Jennifer: NOOOOO!

Georgina: (turns to the worker next to her) So . . . what does your button do?

THE END

Dear Arthur,

Your piece made me laugh out loud. It is really one-sided, but I feel like maybe your quirky writing style might be tricky for others to match. It's great, though. You really went with it and made it work!

Hark

> When are you getting here? What are your plans when you're here?

> Do you want to come for supper one night? Pizza? Ham and pineapple?

> my bus gets in sat am. eating w my dad sun nite. + were watching football sun.

> That's all you've got? Want to hang out Saturday night then? We could go to a movie or just hang out too. Whatever you want to do!

> yeah man, well hang out, u sound like a lovesick girl rite now.

> Shut up.

> dork

> Meathead.

dumass

Oh, do you mean Alexandre Dumas? Because he was famous for being a great French writer. So thank you for the compliment.

u r seriouslly the biggest nerd of all time + i dont know why im ur friend

It's because I'm very clever and handsome and I bring up your cool quotient.

oh ya sure, that must b it

▶▶ ▶▶ ▶▶

October 6th

Dear RJ,

Man, it's cool to have Robbie back in town. We hung out all day yesterday. We played video games and we hung out at the elementary school playground for a bit and we got pizza and we saw a movie. It was epic. I forgot how funny Robbie is in real life. He was imitating all his new teachers and the other guys trying out for the football team. I can't believe that he isn't in Drama at his school. He should be a stand-up comedian. I'm going to ask my dad if I can visit him for Remembrance Day or something. He said that his mom is really strict though and doesn't let him or Caleb leave the house except for "mom-sanctioned activities." He said she calls them "MSAs." It sounds so stupid. No wonder Robbie tried out for football. I would try and spend as much time away from home too if my mom had done something like that. Still, I like the sounds of a vacation, even if it is in Lethbridge.

Yours truly,
Arthur Bean

▸▸ ▸▸ ▸▸

> How was the rest of your trip home? My weekend was lame after we hung out.

Ya, the bus suckd

> Guess what? My dad wants us to do some kind of father-son activity. Like a sport! Me, doing a sport! Ha!

thats got comedy ritten all over it

> First he wanted me to join his yoga class. Ha!

lol

> So now he's letting me choose the activity. What would you choose?

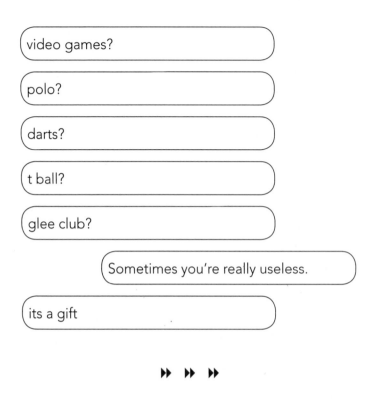

video games?

polo?

darts?

t ball?

glee club?

Sometimes you're really useless.

its a gift

▶▶ ▶▶ ▶▶

From: Arthur Bean (arthuraaronbean@gmail.com)
To: Kennedy Laurel (imsocutekl@hotmail.com)
Sent: October 8, 17:02

Dear Kennedy,

I was thinking of asking you for that favour that you owe me from the fall carnival. Can you write the article about Ms Kraleigh for me? There are a few reasons why.

1) It'll look great on your leadership award application! I'm pretty sure she's in charge of picking the person, so then you can really show her how great you are!

2) I think she might hate me. She definitely doesn't understand my sense of humour. If she brings it up, I wasn't making fun of her shoes by asking if she was going to her bowling league after work. I really thought she was wearing bowling shoes. It was part of my "getting to know you" interview. She didn't take it well.

3) I may have said some things that I shouldn't have when she said that she wanted to make the school a bully-free zone. I just don't think that you get to declare a bully-free zone and *poof!* all bullying is done. Anyway, our conversation may have gone off track at that point, and so maybe you could do it.

Would you mind? I really do think you can make a great impression. Just don't bring up a bully-free zone, or her shoes. She's a little sensitive about those subjects.

Yours truly,
Arthur Bean

▶▶　▶▶　▶▶

From: Kennedy Laurel (imsocutekl@hotmail.com)
To: Arthur Bean (arthuraaronbean@gmail.com)
Sent: October 9, 8:10

Hi Arthur,

I'll do it, but I think we should talk with Mr. E. about whether you're going to screw everything up for the paper. I'm really counting on this award!! And why would you EVER insult a girl's shoes? That's SO not cool!

Kennedy

From: Arthur Bean (arthuraaronbean@gmail.com)
To: Kennedy Laurel (imsocutekl@hotmail.com)
Sent: October 9, 16:27

Dear Kennedy,

Thanks so much! I promise that I'm not trying to
cause any trouble. I think I was just so nervous that I
spoke without thinking. But don't worry. Ms Kraleigh
will never have to deal with me again!

Yours truly,
Arthur Bean

▶▶ ▶▶ ▶▶

October 10th

Dear RJ,

Dad and I are going to start fencing lessons next
week. He wanted me to choose something we
could do together (I think he's been reading the
parenting books my aunt gave him). I figured
that fencing would be the easiest and the coolest.
It's not really a sport, but we get to learn how to
stab people. I watched some videos of fencers,
and it looks pretty cool. Plus, now he'll have to
buy me a sword, which will just be handy to
have around. You never know when you're going
to need to be an expert swashbuckler. Maybe
pirates will overtake our apartment building. Or
maybe the third musketeer will die and I'll be
called up to defend France. Ha!

Thanksgiving is this weekend, so we're spending the weekend in Balzac at my grandparents' house. I don't think Dad wants to go, but thankfully, there will be turkey. Grandma wouldn't hear of having vegetarian Thanksgiving. I think she thinks tofu is poisonous, which is awesome. I hope his vegetarian kick ends soon. At least he buys me deli meat for making my lunch. Otherwise, I would maybe die.

Yours truly,
Arthur Bean

▸▸ ▸▸ ▸▸

Assignment: Literary Devices Summary Story

To improve your writing skills, we are moving forward from individual literary devices to the final assignment in the unit. If you have any questions about material we've covered, please come and see me.

Write a short story of at least one page, incorporating at least three of the literary devices we studied. Challenge yourself to use as many of the following literary devices as you can:

Personification
Onomatopoeia
Similes and Metaphors
Hyperbole
Irony

Please underline any literary devices used in your story.

Due: October 30

▸▸ ▸▸ ▸▸

The Leg Breakers are having a play festival! We're going to write and direct our own shows. Isn't that awesome?

I'm going to start working on my play this week. Can you design the set for me?

I'll give you credit in the program for being the set designer. We could build it at spring break.

My dad can probably help. He belongs to a tool library, so you get to borrow whatever drill or saw you need for the weekend. Maybe your dad will let us use his work garage as a carpentry shop. Can you ask him for me?

i made the football team, thanx for asking

Right! Sorry, I just assumed you did. I figured there was no way you wouldn't.

We can celebrate by building sets at Easter! I can throw some football stuff into the play if you want. 64! 28! Hut!

▶▶ ▶▶ ▶▶

JOGO (Just One Guy's Opinion): School ID Requirements

By Arthur Bean

Ms Kraleigh has made her first mark as principal of Terry Fox Jr. High with a highly controversial decision. As of next Monday, all students must have their student ID visible at all times. The decree came out on Tuesday, when all students were handed their student ID on a bright blue Terry Fox Jr. High lanyard. Any student not wearing their ID will be sent home to retrieve it. And good luck if you're one of those kids who loses everything all the time: lost IDs will cost you $10 each time you need a new one.

I see this new school law as problematic for a number of reasons, but I'm going to focus on two. One: Safety. Ms Kraleigh insists that the IDs are to be worn for our protection, ensuring that everyone in the school belongs in the school. She insists that teachers will also be wearing their IDs. But is it really a great idea to have our names and photos printed on things we can lose so easily? In a world riddled with identity theft, what if someone steals not only my ID but also my identity? There's a lot of information encrypted in those cards; a smart identity thief could probably find out all kinds of personal information if they got their hands on one. Teachers are always talking about how important it is that we keep our identities safe online. Shouldn't the same logic apply to offline?

Two: Fashion. Royal blue may be one of the school colours, but it's not the easiest colour to match. I feel certain that there is a large contingent of the student body who will have to re-think their entire wardrobe. And we know what that means: it means that the office staff will be overworked handing out late passes to every girl who couldn't find the right shoes to go with her lanyard. Poor Mrs. Hui. She's going to have carpal tunnel before winter break! And not just that, but Lucie D'Allard got her braces off one week AFTER picture day. She's stuck with the constant reminder of her dental shortcomings for the whole year. If you ask me, that's just not right. But hey, that's . . .

Just One Guy's Opinion.

Hey, Artie,

This is an interesting start to your editorials. Coming out with a bang, hey?
I think it is important that the newspaper share the student opinion, but we do want to remain objective as well. Come by my class at lunch tomorrow and we'll edit your piece to ensure it's respectful to everyone. We'll make sure that it looks good, and then we can publish your article and Kennedy's pro-ID-wearing article side-by-side. We'll make sure that our readers get to read from both sides of the coin!

Cheers!
Mr. E.

From: Arthur Bean (arthuraaronbean@gmail.com)
To: Robbie Zack (robbiethegreat2000@hotmail.com)
Sent: October 18, 18:43

Dear Robbie,

What are you up to this weekend? I'm not doing much of anything. Other than starting work on my play, of course. I was thinking of writing a five-act play like all of Shakespeare's stuff, but Hark said that he wanted it to be a one-act play festival. I suggested to him that my play could be the final night of the festival, and cap it all off with this epic tragedy. He said that I could write a long show, but that I should challenge myself to write a shorter, tighter piece, but keeping the tension of a long piece. He's totally right, of course. Not only that, but the plays have to be written before Christmas break so that we can cast them and rehearse in the winter. You should transfer back to Calgary for the second semester! You could be in my play! I've been thinking about ways to get football into my show, but I don't know if it's going to happen.

How's football? Are you the quarterback yet?

Yours truly,
Arthur Bean

From: Robbie Zack (robbiethegreat2000@hotmail.com)
To: Arthur Bean (arthuraaronbean@gmail.com)
Sent: October 19, 15:04

Hey dude-

mom is super strict re: w-end screentime (sux so
hard), so this is gonna be short. caleb is losing
his mind w her. its almost funny. lethbridge =
deathbridge = true story. Plus, mom signed up
both me and caleb for tutoring. there goes any fun.
football is good. i'm not QB, just defence mostly.
the guys on the team are pretty cool. theyve all been
going to school 2gether 4 so long tho that i dont get
most of the in-jokes.

   theres 1 girl who i think is cool. her names Hayley
and shes into art. shes hot, but shes pretty quiet. i
think she has a bf tho. Shes always with this guy with
died purple hair named dominic. Im 4ever cursed in
love. just call me shakespear.

Rob

From: Arthur Bean (arthuraaronbean@gmail.com)
To: Robbie Zack (robbiethegreat2000@hotmail.com)
Sent: October 19, 18:19

Dear Robbie,

Hayley sounds awesome. It sucks that she's dating someone already. But you should have an edge, being the new, mysterious football player at the school. There's no one here to date, either.

On another topic, Kennedy got elected to the grad committee. She's really excited. I think she'll do a pretty good job of making it a good party. She's already been coming into the Leg Breakers to get some candid photos of all the clubs for the year-end slideshow. Catie's on the grad committee too. She's as awful and mean as ever, so I try and avoid her at all costs. I can't believe you used to like her last year! I hope that Hayley is a better human.

My dad and I started fencing this week too. It sucks! It was all a bunch of footwork, and we practised going forwards and backwards for an hour, because in fencing you can ONLY go backwards and forwards. You can't even turn your back on your opponent without losing a point. Not only that, but our fencing master (that's what he calls himself) is this French dude named Didier (I call him Deeter), and all the commands and steps are in French. It's really lame, and I asked him to do it in English, but he said that fencing is always in French. It sucks so much, but Dad said that we had to finish the beginner lessons, so I'm stuck until winter break. At least Dad seemed to hate it too. Hate brings families together!

Yours truly,
Arthur Bean

Hey, Artie,

Can you stop by my classroom today after school? Ms Kraleigh and I want to chat with you about your articles.

Cheers!
Mr. E.

October 21st

Dear RJ,

I can't believe it! I got called into a meeting today with the new principal and Mr. Everett to talk about my article about school IDs. Ms Kraleigh thought that it shouldn't be printed, and she wanted to talk about respecting the school policies and the decisions made by those in authority. I told her straight up that I wasn't being disrespectful, but that I thought her new policy was stupid. I couldn't tell what Mr. Everett thought, but I figured he would take my side. After all, he said that I did a good job on my article. We even went over it on Friday together! He was silent through the whole thing, and just said that we would be working on our objectivity. I tried to explain to Ms Kraleigh that I used all the techniques I'd learned in English about writing a persuasive argument, and I figured that that would show her that I was a good student, but she didn't care. Frankly, RJ, she should care. I'm not one who should be getting in trouble. It's not like I'm smoking or skipping school. I bet I'm one of the most boring kids at Terry Fox (well, not more boring than April Rawlin; she is seriously dull). I barely have any friends. I don't know if I'm madder about getting in trouble or what I got in trouble for. I'm the editor. Editors have opinions! That's my job!!! What does she want? A newspaper full of lame articles about sports?

Yours truly,
Arthur Bean

▶▶   ▶▶   ▶▶

Dear Hark,

I started working on my play this weekend, and I wanted to get your opinion on where I started. I want to keep the dramatic tension really high for the whole thing. Can you give me some feedback or pointers on what I have so far?

Yours truly,
Arthur Bean

Draft Outline for Play Festival

By Arthur Bean

Scene One: Living Room
Matt and Chelsey are fighting. They break up, and
Matt leaves.

Scene Two: On the Street
Matt is sad, and on the street. He is confronted by
a gang of six people. He thinks he's going to be
mugged, but instead, they kidnap him and take him
to their secret lair.

Scene Three: The Secret Lair
It turns out the gang is actually a group of
superheroes who need Matt, because Matt is
inadvertently carrying a ring that makes him
indestructible (it used to be his grandfather's ring,
but it's been passed down through the generations).
Matt tests out his new superpower, where the gang
pretends to beat him up, and he is able to stop them.
He learns that he needs to help them defeat The
Great Evil, who is a demon who has risen to destroy
humanity.

Scene Four: The Training Room in the Secret Lair
They train.

Scene Five: The Demon Lair
The team is ready, and they descend into the
demon's lair. The demon and his minions are there,
and there's an epic battle. Matt loses the ring during
the fight, and he ends up in hand-to-hand combat
with the demon, who doesn't know Matt has lost
the ring. Matt and The Great Evil both deliver killing
blows at the same time, and both die. The gang that

is left is relieved, and they return to the surface of earth victorious.

Scene Six: The Living Room
The gang goes to Matt and Chelsey's house to share the sad news of Matt's death. Chelsey is very sad, but accepts Matt's grandfather's ring. Then she says, "I will give this to our baby," and rubs her stomach like she's pregnant.

The End

▶▶ ▶▶ ▶▶

Dear Arthur,

Wow! This IS epic! I can tell that you thought a lot about completing the circle and have a defined conflict, like we talked about. Here's something to consider: you told me about your experience in film; remember how different plays are. Major scene changes are a big problem for staging, and can interrupt the flow and the dramatic tension you're trying to create. Think smaller, and think tighter. What story would you like to tell, and how can you tell it in one space? Consider how you could stage your play. Remember that we can't have too many different sets backstage either; we're all working together here to put on this festival! Creativity is going to be the key to world building!

Otherwise, though, I want to see you develop this into a film script one day. It's going to be amazing!

Hark

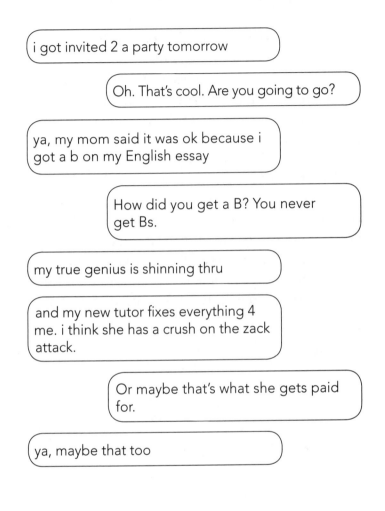

i got invited 2 a party tomorrow

Oh. That's cool. Are you going to go?

ya, my mom said it was ok because i got a b on my English essay

How did you get a B? You never get Bs.

my true genius is shinning thru

and my new tutor fixes everything 4 me. i think she has a crush on the zack attack.

Or maybe that's what she gets paid for.

ya, maybe that too

October 25th

Dear RJ,

It's official. I'm being replaced. Robbie's got his new football friends, and they even invited him to a party this weekend. This means I've got to make some new friends fast. I wonder if Ben is having a party. I should find out who is having a Halloween party. Maybe I should ask Ben to hang out one day. He's in the Leg Breakers too and we make jokes that we both laugh at, so I know we have stuff in common. Or maybe Haruki. But he's only in grade eight. I bet Kennedy is going to a party. I should ask her and then go. I don't think you need to be actually invited to stuff. A party is a party, right?

I wish I got invited to more stuff, RJ. No one ever invites me to parties. I know I'm not a geek, because nobody avoids me at school and they don't make fun of me, but they don't notice me, either. I'm told that you're not supposed to care about what other people think, and I don't, but I do want them to like me and be friends with me.

Yours truly,
Arthur Bean

▶▶ ▶▶ ▶▶

The Trip

By Arthur Bean

Dennis Bruce was a high-powered businessman in the world of insider trading. He <u>wore his Armani suit like a badge of honour</u>, and <u>carried his briefcase like a St. Bernard dog carrying medicine to sick people</u>. People would see him and <u>bam!</u> They fell in love with him. <u>He was the most popular insider trader</u> New York had ever seen. <u>He was a machine</u> when it came to charming people. <u>He was literally</u>

<u>a god on Wall Street</u>. There was even a statue of him in front of his building, which never happens while you're still alive.

Anyway, Mr. Bruce was on his way to the airport to catch his flight to Paris. He had a meeting in the morning with <u>all of the most important people in the world</u>. He had to be there. <u>His absence would be like a missing stitch in the middle of a cable-knit sweater</u>. The whole thing would fall apart.

But here was the thing about Mr. Bruce. He was a superstitious flyer. Mr. Bruce had a few rituals that had to be followed before getting on the plane. First, he had to <u>zip his coat zipper</u> seven times. Then he had to <u>crack four walnuts with his nutcracker</u> and eat them all at once. <u>Since Mr. Bruce was allergic to nuts, he then had to stab himself with his EpiPen in the thigh</u>. And of course, he had to have raspberry yogourt.

Mr. Bruce was waiting in line for the Concord, which annoyed him. He never had to wait in line. <u>He was in super executive first class</u>; he should never have to wait! <u>He was a bundle of anger and nerves</u>, and was about to burst when he realized that he had forgotten his yogourt! Mr. Bruce jumped out of line, <u>and ran as fast as he could</u> down the airport. He stopped in the first gift kiosk he saw. "Do you have yogourt?" They didn't. He swore at them, and tried the next store. They didn't have any, either. He was getting frantic, <u>like a ten-year-old girl waiting for boy band concert tickets to go on sale</u>. Not only that, but they were announcing his name over the intercom; it was last call for his plane and they were going to leave without him. Mr. Bruce started crying. <u>"I will DIE if I don't get raspberry yogourt!"</u> he screamed. <u>He was a puddle on the floor of the airport</u>. With that, a kind vendor came up to him. The vendor handed him a raspberry yogourt. Mr. Bruce sobbed in relief. He tried to pay the man $1000, but the vendor wouldn't take any money. Mr. Bruce began his sprint back to Gate C to catch his plane.

When he got there, there was no one left, and the doors to board were locked. He watched helplessly from the window as his plane taxied away. He <u>zipped his zipper</u> seven times while he clutched his yogourt. He watched the Concord zooming down the runway and lift into the air. <u>BOOM!</u> The plane exploded into a <u>gazillion pieces</u>.

Arthur,

Well done. Your understanding of irony is strong, and I appreciate that you used it twice in your story. You've demonstrated several examples of each literary device here to great effect and yet still maintained a strong plot. There is, however, one spot in your story where you've underlined a simile that is not a simile. See if you can find it!

Ms Whitehead

Dear Ms Whitehead,

I would also like to note that I'm handing my story in two days early. I'm certain no one else in the class is as on top of assignment due dates as I am. I also want to say that I could have covered all of the literary devices in less than six sentences. Mr. Harker said that being brief is the soul of wit, which means my story would have been better if it were shorter.

Yours truly,
Arthur Bean

▶▶ ▶▶ ▶▶

> We actually got to use the real swords tonight.

what were u using before? wrapping paper rolls?

> We weren't using anything! It was all footwork.

i thot u were quitting

> Not yet. Did you know the swords are electric? You have to plug them in to score any points.

so the guy with the longest ex-tension cord wins?

I don't know, actually. We didn't get to fight. Again. Seriously, I thought this could be fun, but it's more like a sport. We just train all the time doing lunges and footwork. Deeter said that next week we'll have our first bouts.

whats that all a bout??

A BOUT?!?!? HAHAHAHA i kill me.

And you think I'm a dork. Do you know how many football puns I could make at your expense?

im guessing you fumbled them?

im on FIRE 2nite!

▶▶ ▶▶ ▶▶

JOGO: Costumes at Halloween

By Arthur Bean

Tomorrow is Halloween, and I want to put it out there that maybe we should all grow up and not wear costumes. I know some of you out there really love dressing up, but I think I speak for the majority when I say, "Enough already!"

Costumes come and go. As kids, we dress up, we get candy. Then we get too old to actually be cute to adults anymore. We could still dress up, but you need a mask to cover your acne-covered face, so what's the point? None of the kids' costumes fit us anymore, and the adult ones look ridiculous. Face it, we're done with costumes until our OWN kids are old enough to be embarrassed by the Mickey Mouse costume we pull out each year to hand out candy.

So let's be cool, guys. Let's leave the Iron Man costumes in the closet for a few years. Feel like you're missing a holiday? Arrival of Indentured Labourers Day is celebrated in Mauritius on November 2nd. We could celebrate that! But hey, that's . . .

Just One Guy's Opinion.

Hey, Artie,

I'm totally opposed to your viewpoint (I've already got a killer costume from ComicCon), but then maybe you think I'm old enough to fit into your "geeky dad" category! On the flip side, I never did find someone to be the second half of my horse costume last year. I hope you don't mind being the voice of the minority; Kennedy's working on a really cool piece about Halloween costumes bringing out a person's true spirit, so these two articles will make for an interesting edition of the Marathon this week!

(On a different note, I never got your heart dissection analysis. Don't forget to bring it to class on Monday!) (I was trying to come up with something heart related to joke about, but it was all in vein . . .)

Cheers!
Mr. E.

From: Arthur Bean (arthuraaronbean@gmail.com)
To: Kennedy Laurel (imsocutekl@hotmail.com)
Sent: October 30, 19:40

Dear Kennedy,

Are you going to any great Halloween parties? I'm totally torn about which one to go to!
   You probably thought I wouldn't go to any parties because of my article, but I loved reading the draft of your article about Halloween costumes. It made a lot of sense. So now I'm back on board with Halloween. So let me know what you're going to be up to, and maybe I'll see you around this weekend!

Yours truly,
Arthur Bean

▶▶ ▶▶ ▶▶

From: Kennedy Laurel (imsocutekl@hotmail.com)
To: Arthur Bean (arthuraaronbean@gmail.com)
Sent: October 31, 17:05

Hey Arthur,

Enjoy your parties! I don't think I'm going to do anything tonight or this weekend. I never really heard about anything going on. It's so stupid, but sometimes I think that I only get invited to things because Catie invites me. Maybe no one else likes me.
   I'm only kidding. Don't mind me. I'm just annoyed because I didn't make the senior volleyball team, and I just found out. So it's probably good that I'm not

going out this weekend. I'm going to stay home and wallow in candy and bad movies LOL!

Kennedy ☺

From: Arthur Bean (arthuraaronbean@gmail.com)
To: Kennedy Laurel (imsocutekl@hotmail.com)
Sent: October 31, 17:57

Dear Kennedy,

I would have made you captain of the team. I can't believe you didn't make it! Do you want me to write an article about the shady recruitment practices for the school sports teams? I bet there's a lot of dirt to dig up!
    If you want some company, I could come hang out.

Yours truly,
Arthur Bean

October 31st

Dear RJ,

No response from Kennedy. What does that mean? Why didn't she respond yet? Should I text her with the same stuff? I never text her, so that might be weird. But why didn't she respond? I ALWAYS respond to emails.
    You know what? It's fine. I don't care. (Maybe if I write that enough it will become true.)

Yours truly,
Arthur Bean

NOVEMBER

From: Von Ipo (thenexteastwood@hotmail.com)
To: Arthur Bean (arthuraaronbean@gmail.com)
Sent: November 1, 18:03

Hey, Artie!

LOVED your article about costumes. I am in total agreement with you, man. I hate coming up with a costume every year.

Anyways, I was wondering if you have Kennedy's number. I wanted to text her and ask her to be in my play. I don't know if she'll do it, she might be too busy with grad committee. Actually, you know what? I'll ask her at our meeting next week. I don't know why more guys didn't run for grad committee. I'm totally outnumbered there. Not that I mind. The chicks are so hot!

What's your play about? I'm thinking that mine will be about the illuminati, or maybe about terrorists. Maybe we could hang out and I could help you come up with a cool idea. Let me know. I've got hockey this weekend, but I'm around Sunday night.

Von

▶▶ ▶▶ ▶▶

From: Arthur Bean (arthuraaronbean@gmail.com)
To: Robbie Zack (robbiethegreat2000@hotmail.com)
Sent: November 4, 18:11

Dear Robbie,

I don't know why I'm writing. I didn't do anything this weekend. There's nothing new happening here. How was your party?

I'm supposed to do homework, but instead I was looking up fencing rules online. Did you know that there's no slashing in fencing? Well, there actually is, but Deeter is only teaching us foil. There are three different types of fencing, and we only get to try the hardest one. It's so much work, and foil fencing is so picky. You have to hit your opponent only in the chest for it to count for anything. Not only that, but my dad makes us take the bus to the gym because you have to pay for parking there, so then after we are definitely the smelliest guys on the bus. I hate smelling bad. It's one of the top reasons that I don't do sports.

How was your Halloween party? There weren't any parties at all this year. It's always that way when Halloween is on a weekday. Was Hayley there? Did you talk to her?

Did your team make the football provincials? It'd be cool if you got to come up to Calgary with your team. I would even come to your game. I could interview you too, because I need someone with football knowledge for a story I want to write. It isn't really about football. It's about a group of girl cheerleaders who kill the school quarterback.

See? This is how bored I am. I'm writing stories where you are the protagonist. Talk about desperate!!

Yours truly,
Arthur Bean

▶▶ ▶▶ ▶▶

Assignment: Novel Study — Dystopian Fiction

Calling all *Hunger Games* fans! Our group novel study will focus on the dystopian genre.

You have a choice: you can read *The Chrysalids* by John Wickham, *How I Live Now* by Meg Rosoff, or *House of the Scorpion* by Nancy Farmer. I don't want to hear any complaints: I've chosen these books based on the reading surveys you filled in last week! Each novel's specifics will give us a lot to discuss in class, so I expect you to actively participate in class debates.

The setting of a dystopian novels often focuses on a utopian vision for society, a vision that has gone wrong.

In a paragraph or two, describe what utopia is to you, and reflect upon how that could become a dystopia.

Due: November 12

▶▶ ▶▶ ▶▶

Did you guys get today off too? It's so weird to be off on a Monday.

ya we're off but im meeting some of the guys to practice cuz our playoff game is sat

Cool! I bet you'll win.

i dout it the other teams relly good

Maybe my dad will want to drive down and we can watch it. It's not like I'm doing anything this weekend!

ya if u want

What else is new? School here kind of sucks. The new principal hates me. I've decided to hate her on principle. Ha! Get it?

Maybe I'll go to a movie. Have you seen anything recently?

Oh yeah. And Catie started dating Jeff Wong but then she kissed his stepbrother and Jeff saw it and he dumped her. So she's pretending to be heartbroken and running out of class crying all the time. I think she's just found a way to get out of French.

No response?

I guess you already went to practice.

I'm basically talking to myself then.

Well, then, I say, Arthur, old chap, you are a smashing gent.

(I was probably a British gentleman in a past life.)

Well, I have to go too. I'll let you know if we can come down for the weekend!

⏩ ⏩ ⏩

Assignment: My Utopia

By Arthur Bean

My idea of utopia is a world where everyone gets a chance to express their opinion without getting shot down by those in charge; this would be number one. I think that school would only happen four days a week, and no one would be super poor or super rich. In my utopia, there would be libraries without late fines. I would also get rid of bedbugs, because they creep me out; my old next-door neighbour Nicole got bedbugs in her suitcase while she was travelling, and then they infested her house and she got bitten everywhere; it was so gross that I didn't want to sit down anywhere when we went to visit her. Since I'm getting rid of things, I would get rid of mosquitoes too; I don't see the point of keeping them around. And fruit flies; they can go too.

I was going to say that there would be no death in my utopia, but that's crazy and definitely one way to make the world a dystopia; in fact, I thought of so many things that would make the world better, but I looked up utopia in the dictionary and it said that it actually means "no place," so it can never really exist; I think that's why my utopia is a dystopia. It just gets people's hopes up that life will be perfect, and I can say with total certainty that that's just not true.

Arthur,

I'm pleased to see that you took some extra time to research the word. On the whole, you start off strong, looking at global qualities, rights and freedoms, but you take a wrong turn when you focus on minor qualities like bedbugs. The story about your neighbour is unnecessary, and it doesn't add to your argument. Remember to stay focused on the task at hand, and to develop your ideas with more insight and reflection on why those things would make for a better world.

Also, I appreciate that you are practising your use of the semi-colon, but remember that it isn't always the best type of punctuation to use. A good writer uses a variety of sentence lengths to keep the reader engaged. There's nothing wrong with having short sentences!

▶▶ ▶▶ ▶▶

November 16th

Dear RJ,

I had asked Dad if we could go to Lethbridge
for the weekend to see Robbie play football,
but we couldn't because he had signed up for
a silent meditation practice. Like he needs to
practise being silent. The guy barely talks as
it is! So instead, I am stuck at home, AGAIN.
I complained, but Dad said that I should go
out and do something. I reminded him that
generally fourteen-year-olds don't hang around
outside by themselves, and not only that, it's
windy and rainy and minus a thousand outside.
So he convinced me to go to the movies by
myself.

WORST IDEA EVER. Dad said that it would
be fine and that no one would know because the
movie theatre was dark. But as soon as I walked
in, Kennedy and Catie were there, right in front
of me in line! I thought about pretending not
to see them, but as soon as Kennedy turned
around, I couldn't very well ignore her. She
asked who I was there with, and I couldn't think
of someone fast enough, so I said that I was
there with my cousin Luke. Then she got all
excited, and said that she had never met Luke
and asked if we wanted to sit with them. I said
that we probably weren't going to see the same
movie. So she asked what movie. And the only
options at the matinee were the new Avengers
movie, some kind of weird biopic about a guy
from Denmark and an old people's romantic
comedy starring a bunch of eighty-year-olds

reliving their youth on a bus tour (remind me, RJ, to only make good movies when I'm famous). Kennedy looked confused, so I said, "We're going to the old people movie."

She laughed and asked me why, and I couldn't come up with anything good, so I repeated a line that my mom used to say all the time. "Because I love Diane Keaton," I said. "She's underappreciated as an actor, but she's got the chops."

RJ, I don't even know what that means! I was so nervous. Catie gave me a look like I was the loserest (not a word, I know) person ever. And then I had to buy my ticket while they were standing beside me, so I got two tickets to the old person movie. And then Kennedy asked if Luke was in the bathroom since I was buying two tickets, so I had to say yes. So there we were, the three of us, waiting in the lobby for a guy who was never going to show up. After ten minutes, Catie lost it and said that they were going to miss the previews, and I said, "Luke must have diarrhea," and Kennedy looked totally disgusted, but said, "I hope he's okay." I'm sure that Catie didn't believe me though. She has a sixth sense for that kind of thing. So they left, and then I was going to sneak into the Avengers after the previews and grab a seat, but I looked in and it was totally sold out. I had nothing to do for two hours until my dad came to get me, so I ended up watching the stupid old-person movie anyway. Diane Keaton sure can cry on cue.

All this to say that I just spent double the price

on a movie I didn't want to see, and Kennedy
thinks that my family is either imaginary or
suffering from disgusting stomach problems
and that I have the same taste in movies as a
grandmother. Really great, Arthur. That's the
way to make an impression. I knew I should
have stayed home.

Yours truly,
Arthur Bean

▶▶ ▶▶ ▶▶

November 18th

Dear RJ,

We went to fencing tonight, and I didn't even
complain because there are only three sessions
left. But, RJ, there were new people at fencing
tonight! And not lame fifty-year-olds, either,
but real people! These two girls who are both in
grade nine. One of them even goes to my school!
I've seen Camille (or I guess she goes by Millie? I
never knew that) around, but we've never really
talked. And her friend Joie (she pronounces
it Joey) is in the French school, but she's not
French, she's Vietnamese (and apparently a lot
of Vietnamese people speak French; who knew?).
They said that they normally fence on Tuesday
and Thursday nights, and that I should join their
class because it's way more fun. They are a bit
weird in a kind of crazy way, and I didn't really
get most of their jokes, but they were nice to me.

Do you think that means that they both like me? I hope not. I don't want to ruin their friendship. But if one of them was going to like me, I hope it's Millie. Then Kennedy would see us together and get really jealous. Anyway, having them at fencing made the class way more fun. They really get into the theatrics of the bouts, and I think they're actually pretty good fencers too, which makes sense; they've been fencing for four years! It was so much better tonight having people to joke around with, RJ. Plus they made fun of Deeter to his face and he just laughed it off. So maybe fencing isn't so bad.

Yours truly,
Arthur Bean

▶▶ ▶▶ ▶▶

JOGO: Phones at Lunch

By Arthur Bean

The Terry Fox Jr. High administration has come down with another bizarre rule: no cell phones in the lunch room. Ms Kraleigh has decreed that the school is a place of learning and that cell phones being used during lunch promote cyber-bullying and lessen social inter-actions. Apparently, our phones are to stay in our lockers during school hours. Sure, I'll give it to her that cell phones in class shouldn't be allowed. Just because you can look something up doesn't mean that you shouldn't learn it in the first place. But extending the no phones policy to the lunch break? Why? I don't see what the harm in having cell phones for an hour of the day could be. What if we have friends in other cities who are dying to know how we did on that tricky Math quiz? Or what if a fight breaks out about which Teenage Mutant Ninja Turtle carried which weapon, and the only way to make peace is to look it up? Worse yet, I don't think Ms Kraleigh is looking at the darker side of this debate: What would happen if we ever have an emergency in the school? Leaving cell phones in our lockers does us no good. That's why the majority of us have cell phones, isn't it? In fact, lunch is when we are most at risk! More than 10,000 children end up in the emergency room each year because they choked on something, and 17% of these incidents are on hot dogs alone! You know how I know this? I LOOKED IT UP ON MY PHONE. But hey, that's . . .

Just One Guy's Opinion.

Hey, Artie,

We need to chat about taking on Ms Kraleigh and the school administration in such an aggressive manner, before your piece is final. I appreciate that you are putting some thought into your editorials, but you need to work on the tone of them. I'm not saying that I want you to feel like a "phoney," but let's chat about how we can get your thoughts across in a calmer, more objective manner.

Cheers!
Mr. E.

▶▶   ▶▶   ▶▶

I've tried calling you a couple of times this week. Did you guys win?

sorry man. been busy. didnt win, but we will next yr!

Oh that sucks. It's a good thing that we didn't come down to watch then.

ya i guess, u missed a cool party tho. my whole school was there, even hayley

Did you talk to her?

ya, shes cool. she thinks i should get a job so i can have freedom

Freedom from what? You're not in jail. You're in Lethbridge.

same diffrence dude. plus if i start working now, i can get a car next summer

Then you can visit and drive me places! I fully support this car idea. I'll start thinking about places you can apply. Do you want me to write your resumé?

ya sure. make sure i sound awesome

not that thats hard, cuz im pretty much perfect hahaha

From: Arthur Bean (arthuraaronbean@gmail.com)
To: Robbie Zack (robbiethegreat2000@hotmail.com)
Sent: November 24, 14:52

Dear Robbie,

I started working on a resumé for you and I looked up a bunch of ideas on the Internet, but you have to have had jobs for all the resumés I saw. Did you ever volunteer for anything? I thought you could put our movie on there, since it's probably the biggest thing you've ever committed to before. And you need references, like old bosses and stuff. I figured you could use me as one of your references, since I know you so well, and I'm a pretty trustworthy guy.

Have you thought about what kind of job you want to get? I figured you'd want something with art or football involved. The comic book shop in the mall is hiring for Christmas right now. Maybe you could move back and work there!

Yours truly,
Arthur Bean

From: Robbie Zack (robbiethegreat2000@hotmail.com)
To: Arthur Bean (arthuraaronbean@gmail.com)
Sent: November 24, 17:09

dude u didnt have to write it now. i thot i would get a job with an application form. and i only can work during the summer. my mom doesnt want me working and failing school.

but ill be back during xmas break. calebs not coming back at all. he met some girl and now hes "in love". he doesnt want to leave durring the break. dad is mad. (haha, im such a poet). i dont even know who would want to date caleb! she must be so desperat!

rob

▶▶ ▶▶ ▶▶

Dear Hark,

Here's my play for the Leg Breakers festival. I took your advice and made sure that the cast was small, and that there was only one setting. I tried to keep the tension really high too, so let me know if it's too tense. I wanted to make it tense but funny. I just watched Lethal Weapon with my dad, and I wanted it to be kind of like that, but still really different and more interesting at the end. Do you ever watch really old movies? I generally don't like old movies, but this one was pretty good.
I can't wait to hear what you think! I really hope you like it!

Yours truly,
Arthur Bean

I, Spy
A Play in One Act

By Arthur Bean

Characters:
7 spies (1 is the captain, and two have to look alike)
Setting: A secret location, inside a locked room
(The captain is in the room, setting up the chairs and looking through secret documents. His cell phone rings.)

Captain: Hello? . . . Yes, sir? . . . I'm about to find out, sir? . . . I've called them to a meeting? . . . I'm certain we will find him? . . . Yes, sir. Him or her? . . . Him or her . . . I'll report back soon. *(He hangs up, and smiles mysteriously.)*
(There is a knock at the door. The captain goes over, punches in a key code and the door opens. There are two spies at the door. They salute.)
Captain: Put down your guns and fake IDs on this table and state your name and spy number. *(They both put down their guns and badges.)*
Spy One: My name is Serpentine, number 58008. I think I should keep my gun. It has high-tech laser pointers attached, which are helpful for finding enemies, but also great when called upon to do a powerpoint presentation.
Spy Two: My name is Rat-ical, number 007. My gun is actually four guns in one. I got it from the Swiss Army. It also has nail clippers!
Captain: No guns on your person. I don't care if they are Swiss. I am Captain Subtle. Sit down—there are three more spies coming.
Serpentine: Sir? Can you tell us a little about why we're here? Fill in the back story a little? Rat-ical has a very bad short-term memory.
Captain: Right. I forgot that Rat-ical was involved

in the memory serum debacle. Well, as you know, we've been trying to overthrow the newest dictator here in Canada in 2033. As the resistance, we've been successful on two of our four missions. But if we lose this fifth mission, it's all over and we'll all be executed . . . *(He is interrupted by two more spies entering the room, laughing at a joke between them.)*

Captain *(yelling)*: Excuse me—what are you doing?

Spy Three *(turns to Spy Four)*: Who's he? *(Points to Captain.)*

Spy Four *(aside)*: Can you be a bit more subtle?

Captain: No he can't. Because I am Captain Subtle, you fools. Put your weapons down and sit—you're late.

(Spy Three takes his gun out and tries to put it on the table; his gun is so big with many attachments that he fumbles with it for a while, then ends up just putting it on the floor. Spy Four pretends to put his gun down, but actually puts his gun back inside his jacket when no one is looking. It sticks out, but he pulls the jacket overtop of the gun to camouflage it. They both sit down.)

Serpentine *(to Spy Three and Four)*: Who are you?

Spy Three: I'm Pink Panther and he is Mauve Maverick.

Spy Four: No—I'm Pink Panther and HE is Mauve Maverick.

Spy Three: You said I could be Pink Panther!

Spy Four: No—you wanted to be Mauve Maverick because you like the movie *Top Gun*.

Captain: ENOUGH! We have a mission to accomplish! *(There is silence.)* Good. Now, as I was saying, six spies have been chosen to carry out our fifth and final mission. But I fear that one of us is a mole!

Spy Three: A mole? I'm a panther! A PINK panther. *(He says this pointedly at Spy Four.)*

Serpentine: Well, that guy is a rat! Rats are very

closely related to moles. I think.

Rat-ical: Are you suggesting that I work for the enemy? I'll fight you!

Captain: STOP! You've all realized by now that one of us is the enemy. I called you all here so that we can figure out who it is and get rid of him so that we succeed.

Spy Four: Do you mean . . . kill them?

Spy Three: That's a little harsh.

Spy Four: I'm sure a stern talking to would be enough.

Captain: SHUT UP, YOU FOOLS! Now, who is the mole?

Serpentine: Well, it's not me.

Rat-ical: Exactly what a mole would say.

Captain: I agree with Serpentine. Rat-ical looks like a mole.

Spy Three: Well then, it's settled. Rat-ical is a mole. We can leave now.

Rat-ical: I am not a mole! I'm a *rat*!

Serpentine: So rats *aren't* moles? Then I think that it's YOU! *(Points to Spy Three.)*

Spy Three: That's preposterous! Just ask Mauve Maverick. I've been with the resistance the last fourteen years. What would even make you think I'm a mole?

Serpentine: You're accusing another. You're trying to shift blame!

Rat-ical: It's like the old saying: he who smelt it . . .

Serpentine and **Rat-ical** (*together*): DEALT IT.

Spy Four: What? Someone farted?

Captain (*under his breath*): Excuse me.

Spy Three: Let's vote on who the mole is.

Captain: Good idea. If you think Serpentine is the mole, put up your hands. *(No one does.)*

Serpentine: Good. I'm glad you believe in me.

Captain: If you think Rat-ical is the mole, put up

your hands. *(Captain Subtle and Spy Three put up their hands.)*

Captain: If you think Pink Panther . . .

Spy Four: Mauve Maverick.

Captain: Whatever. That guy *(points to Spy Three)* is the mole . . . *(Rat-ical and Serpentine put up their hands.)*

Captain: Wait a minute. *(Turns to Spy Four.)* You haven't voted yet, and you're the only one left. Are you giving yourself up?

Spy Four: I'm not the only one left. There's also you, Captain Subtle.

Spy Three *(mutters)*: Ooooh. Subtle. I should have seen that coming. It's so obvious.

Captain: That's absurd. How can I be the mole AND lead the mission?

Spy Four: I know it's you! *(Pulls his gun on Captain Subtle.)*

Captain: I told you to put your weapons on the table!

Spy Four: Sit down. *(Captain sits down.)* Let me explain. I am from the future.

Rat-ical: That's impossible!

Spy Four *(continues)*: I was the head of a time-travelling mission and I saw how Captain Subtle will flub the mission on purpose and we will lose.

Spy Three: Wait a minute! I think you, Mauve Maverick, are the mole! None of this makes any sense! You were part of the human-into-animals project, not the time-travelling project. You're lying to us. You're the mole! I'll prove it! *(Goes up to Spy Four and pulls up his pant leg to reveal a paw instead of a foot.)*

Rat-ical: I'm so lost.

Spy Four: I was part of BOTH projects. I got this animal leg after my original leg was blown off in World War Four. I'm telling you, Captain Subtle is the mole! *(Waves his gun wildly.)*

Captain: Prove it. If you can prove it, you can shoot me dead.

Serpentine: Ooh. This just got interesting.

(The door flies open and a spy that looks exactly like Spy Four enters the room.)

New Spy: Sorry I'm late. Traffic was terrible on Sussex Drive. And you know how bad Wellington can be during rush hour. (*He stops and looks around. Spy Four has his gun pointed at Spy Three. Captain Subtle is standing near the weapons table.*) What the . . .

Spy Three: Who are you?

New Spy: I'm Pink Panther. I was called to a meeting.

Spy Four: It's *me*! I'm *here*! There's your proof, Captain!

(Captain Subtle grabs a gun from the table. He shoots and wounds Spy Four. New Spy shoots back, but misses. Serpentine tackles the captain and there is chaos onstage, but eventually Captain Subtle is bound and gagged.)

Serpentine: Problem solved.

Spy Four (*weakly*): Not really . . . (*They all look over and realize that he's dying.*)

New Spy: Wait—you're *me*?!? *I'm* dying?!?

Spy Three (*sobbing*): Mauve Maverick, I love you, man. Don't die . . .

Spy Four (*weakly*): Not . . . Mauve Maverick . . . I . . . wanted to be . . . Pink . . . Pant . . . (*Dies.*)

New Spy: Wait—that was me *in the future*?? I just DIED?!?

Serpentine: I'm afraid so. But the good news is that we solved the pest problem. You know, got rid of the mole.

New Spy: But I *died*! That's it. I'm retiring before this can actually happen. (*Walks out.*)

Rat-ical: I'm glad I'm not a mole.

(There is a knock on the door. Another spy walks in.)

Ever Newer Spy: Oh good. You're all here. I'm

your captain. I've called you here to discuss our new mission. The only problem is that one of us is a mole.
Serpentine: Not again!
(*Blackout.*)

Hi, Arthur!

This is truly amazing. You've done a real bang-up job here. There's tension, there's some real laugh-out-loud moments, and there's even a bit of pathos. I love it!

You may have some trouble with your casting; having two characters who look like each other can be very tricky, especially in a small school. (Look at Shakespeare's Comedy of Errors. So many twins!) Also, getting an animal leg might be a bit tricky in the props/costume department!

You're a bit ahead of the rest of the gang on getting your script in, but I'm hoping that we'll have auditions in a couple of weeks so that we can get to rehearsing as soon as winter break is over.

Cheers!
Hark

▶▶ ▶▶ ▶▶

November 29th

Dear RJ,

I saw Millie at school today and she told me
again that I should join her and Joie's fencing
class in the new year. They are actually going
to competitions, and she said that if I act like
I'm really into fencing, Deeter will let me fence
more bouts, which is way more fun than all
the exercises of parrying and lunging. I want to
fight. That's what I joined for. Plus, this week
Deeter was showing us this really cool move
where you can flick your wrist, and make the
sword bend and tap your opponent's back. It
looks awesome. I tried it on my dad, but I flicked
it too hard and my sword went flying and hit the
guy beside me. I thought it was pretty funny,
but the guy next to me did not.

Anyway, I think I will keep going. It's fun to
hang out with those girls. I definitely think Joie
has a crush on me. She always leans on me
when we're in line until she would fall over if I
were to move. I wonder what Kennedy would say
to that! Ha!

I told Millie that she should be in my play
for Leg Breakers, and she said that she'd do it. I
want to ask Kennedy to be in it too. I think she
would be a really good spy, but I don't know if
she'll do it. Things are so weird with her. I wish
we were friends again. Maybe being in my play
will make that happen. Whenever I see her at
newspaper meetings, all she can talk about is
planning the grad prom or this dumb leadership
award. I actually think I prefer emailing her,

because she's so much nicer to me over email. I have to keep telling her that her article ideas are kind of boring. No one wants fashion advice from the Home Ec. Club!

At least I'm looking at issues that are important to everyone in the school. Sure, Ms Kraleigh doesn't like it, but real journalists tell the truth, and they sometimes get in trouble for it. Plus, she's so strict. My mom used to complain about how strict my elementary school principal was. Mom used to say that principals should be seen but not heard. I used to overhear her complaining about school policies to my dad after I'd gone to bed, and she would say that she couldn't do anything to change them. But I've seen enough documentaries to know that it only takes one person to stand up to a bully before the rest of the world will follow him. I need to be a leader here.

Yours truly,
Arthur Bean

DECEMBER

Assignment: Book Review

The Call of the Wild
by Jack London

I know you're making us write about some of the books we read, so I thought I would do one now. Look at me; I'm so proactive! I should probably get extra bonus marks for not leaving it until the end.

I asked my dad what his favourite book was. He said that right now, his favourite book was by some guy with the strangest name ever: Eckhart Tolle (I had to look that up to spell it right; that should get me bonus marks too). I looked at his books, but they looked terrible and boring. Then Dad said that he has always really loved Jack London's books. So I read *The Call of the Wild*.

As you know, Ms Whitehead, I don't like books with animals as the main characters. I'm not really an animal lover. I barely tolerate my own cat, Pickles. She hates me too, so the feeling is mutual. She was more my mom's cat, but now my dad and I have her around. I'll probably cry when she dies because we've had her so long, but I won't miss the fact that she's half-demon and probably wants to kill me. Anyway, enough about Pickles. *The Call of the Wild* is about a dog who lives the high life in California, but he gets dognapped and taken to the Yukon to be a sled dog and then ends up becoming a wolf.

I was wary when I started this book, because

Buck (the dog) is the main character. I thought maybe he would start talking to rats and other dogs and stuff, and we all know: DOGS DON'T TALK. But then, I kind of got into the book, because Buck doesn't talk, but he does have feelings and thoughts, but he's still a dog. Plus, the plot was really interesting and had a lot of action in it. I really liked Buck and Thornton together, and I was glad that Buck finally found a guy who understood him and didn't abuse him. I don't like Pickles, but I would never hurt her. I don't understand people who do that to animals.

After reading *The Call of the Wild* by Jack London, I've decided that I still don't really like books with animals as the main characters, but I did like this book and I'm glad I read it and not Eckhart Tolle. I also want to go camping in the Yukon. It sounded like it's really awesome up there, so I'm going to ask my dad if we can go one day. I might read *White Fang* too, which is another Jack London book that takes place in the Yukon. I would rate this book eight out of ten (it lost two points because it was about animals).

Yours truly,
Arthur Bean

Arthur,

Thank you for handing in your reading response early. I hope this is the beginning of a new trend for you! I'm glad you enjoyed The Call of the Wild. I've never read it, but maybe I will now that it's been recommended. As you know, I don't really like animal books either, so we're on the same page. I had a similar experience, though, when I read Watership Down. It's an animal book without being like any other animal book. It might pique your interest; let me know if you would like to borrow my copy.

I hope you and your dad get to go to the Yukon; I've seen photos and it looks stunning.

One note: you refer to the plot as being "interesting." Interesting is a boring adjective; it doesn't convey any sense of what something actually is. Next time, try to use words that evoke more emotion!

Ms Whitehead

▸▸ ▸▸ ▸▸

You'll never believe who Kennedy is dating now!!

if u say u, i will come up there and beat sense into u

Ha! Right! I'm so not interested in Kennedy. I just have to work with her on the paper, so I see her a lot.

Trust me, I'm not dating her. I wouldn't even want to. Even if she begged me.

Unless she seriously changed and stopped hanging out with Catie.

Then I would maybe consider it. But until then . . . NO WAY!

r u done yet?

Well, if you're going to be like that, then I won't tell you.

good! i dont care

Fine.

im home for Christmas on the 20th. r u going to be in calgary?

Yeah. We're home for the first bit, then we're going to Balzac to see my grandparents. Boring, but Luke's family's going too!

JOGO: Why Only Dances?

By Arthur Bean

Terry Fox Jr. High often celebrates milestones in the school year with dances. We had a Fall Dance to celebrate Thanksgiving. We have a Winter Dance to celebrate all the different holidays in December. We dance at Valentine's Day, at Spring Equinox and again at the end of the year. My question is: What about the people who hate dancing?

There are many awkward students out there who can't dance. Maybe they don't feel the music deep in their souls. Maybe it's more serious than that, and they have a heart murmur so they can't understand the regularity of a beat. But these poor students have to make a difficult choice each and every time we host a dance: Do they go to the dance and make fools of themselves, or do they stay home and be considered losers?

And a tough choice it is: if they go, they either look ridiculous on the dance floor and everyone laughs at them, or they stand on the side, feeling small and self-conscious. If they don't go, they come off as being anti-school spirit, and they don't get the chance to see their peers socially and make new friends.

Dances are for the popular kids to show off their popularity, and for less popular kids to feel terrible about themselves. It's all about the circle of dancers in the middle of the floor, and who is slow dancing with whom at the end of the night.

So why can't we have different events to celebrate? Instead of a Grad Dance, maybe we should have a grad science expo? Or a grad poetry reading? A grad mathlete nerd-off? Everyone loves scavenger hunts. Why not one of those? I think we should host events that reach a wide range of talents and abilities, not just dances. But hey, that's . . .

Just One Guy's Opinion.

(Note to Readers: I'm actually not a terrible dancer, and I'm not a loser who hangs out along the wall. I just want to speak up for those who are too scared to do so.)

Hey, Artie,

I'm intrigued by your choice of subject this month. I don't know if we want to publish this right before the Winter Waltz, especially since Kennedy and the rest of the committee have worked really hard on planning it. Even though you should call me Ted (because I love Danson! Ted . . . Danson! Get it?), I think you raise some valid points. How about we look at adding a little "pro-dance" paragraph to show you've thought about the counter-argument?

Cheers!
Mr. E.

▶▶ ▶▶ ▶▶

December 12th

Dear RJ,

Against my better judgment, I went to the Winter Waltz tonight. It was so lame, as expected! At least Hark was there, so I got a chance to tell him about my ideas for my next play that I want to write. (It takes place underwater. It's a show about SCUBA diving, and this guy who is about to die because he doesn't have enough oxygen to get back up to the surface, but while he drifts farther down in the water, he discovers all these crazy things that could change the future of the world for the better. But, of course, he dies.) It's got a strong environmental message, which

Hark said sounded amazing. It was too bad that Von came over and joined our conversation. He started talking about all the great things he's supposedly done over the years, and how he and I should get together and write more screenplays. Hark is so nice to him. It must be hard to be a teacher and have to be nice to kids that you actually can't stand. I feel like I'd be terrible at it, because if I was Von's teacher, I would fail him on everything, and give him detention just for being annoying.

Kennedy came up to talk to me too, and I thought at first she was going to ask me to dance, but she said that she couldn't believe I would write an anti-dance article. I tried to explain that it wasn't anti-dance, it was just a suggestion to add some variety in our social events, but she was so mad that she wouldn't listen. I don't know why she has to take everything so personally. I wasn't attacking her! I tried to find her later to apologize, since I figured that it was better to apologize than explain, but she was with Catie all night, so there wasn't any point. I'll try and explain again another time. I wish she would see that I'm way more fun to hang out with than Catie. And I'm nicer too. I'm nice to everybody!

Yours truly,
Arthur Bean

▶▶ ▶▶ ▶▶

I saw an ad for an illustrator today. It's for a graphic design company in Calgary. You should work for them!

dude im 14. im not looking 4 a career

They might have an internship. You'd get to draw all day!

pretty sure that interns make coffee + dont get pd. i want $$$

They have a writer position too. I'm going to apply. We could work together!

i m connstantly impressed by ur cluelesness

I think they will like that I am so in touch with the youth, being one myself.

Ha! more like out to lunch!

which is what ill be if u get me an intern job.

I don't get it.

cuz ill be fetching sandwiches all day

▶▶ ▶▶ ▶▶

Assignment: Winter Break Excuses

Your assignment over the break is to come up with a convincing story as to why you couldn't get any of your homework done!

Put your storytelling abilities and persuasive writing skills to the test, and write me a short story detailing what happened to you to hinder your homework completion and explaining why you should get an extension on your assignment. What makes your situation "extenuating circumstances"? Why should you get special treatment?

Due: January 7

▶▶ ▶▶ ▶▶

December 17th

Dear RJ,

We had auditions today at Leg Breakers for our plays, and I think mine is going to be awesome. Hark had us do auditions inside the playwriting group, and then we opened it up to other people who wanted to be in our plays. Millie actually came to audition like she said she would, so I gave her the part of Serpentine. Ben's going to be Captain Subtle, because he's so tall he'll be imposing and he's so funny and deadpan. I think he'll kill at it. Latha and her little sister Bhakti are playing the time travellers, which will be amazing, because they look so similar, except Bhakti is shorter. Von literally BEGGED me to be in my show, so I kind of had to cast him as a spy. I was hoping that Kennedy would show up, because I think she would be a really funny Rat-ical, but she didn't come. I chose Julia instead, since I'm going to be in her play too. I'm going to be in another play as well. I'm in Julia's as the dad (hers is about a girl who goes to juvenile detention), and in Vincent's as one of the mutant slayers. I have more lines in Vincent's play, but it's shorter. I don't really do much in Julia's, but I do get to yell "Damn it, Beyoncé!" (that's the name of the girl who goes to juvie. I guess Julia's big into her music), and I have to pretend to be drunk and start crying.

I haven't read all our scripts, but I think they sound pretty awesome. Although, I have to admit, RJ, mine is probably the best. Some of them don't really go anywhere (like Julia's). (Don't tell her I said that.)

We're not starting rehearsals until after the break, but I'm going to get off-book, which Hark says is theatre-speak for memorizing all our lines, before we even start. I asked my cast to do the same, so that we can work on making the fight scenes look super realistic.

Yours truly,
Arthur Bean

▶▶ ▶▶ ▶▶

home sweet home

Are you free tonight? Tomorrow?

ya both

Ok. Do you want to come here or do you want me to come there?

i should probly stay w my dad since i just got here. why dont u come here?

Sounds good! On my way!

▶▶ ▶▶ ▶▶

December 21st

Dear RJ,

We had the weirdest night last night! I went to Robbie's apartment, or I guess I should say, Robbie's dad's apartment. Robbie and I hung out and he showed me a bunch of the comics he's been working on. They look awesome. He said that Hayley has been taking his characters and putting them into the oil paintings that she likes to do. He had a few photos of it and he looked super proud of them. I didn't get it at all. It was like the cartoon guys that Robbie draws stuck inside these super realistic fruit bowls and prairie flower landscape things. Some of them were kind of funny though. One had a werewolf trapped under a banana. Robbie also gave me one of me and him where we both look like James Bond in tuxedoes and with guns. It's so awesome. I'm going to frame it.

That's not the weird part. We hung out like normal, but when my dad came to get me, Robbie's dad told me to invite him in for a beer. It was very strange. I don't think they had ever really even met. My dad looked super uncomfortable, and I could tell that he just wanted to leave. Plus, my dad works in a bank, and Robbie's dad is in construction or something, so I don't know what they talked about. Especially since my dad barely talks to people he knows, and not at all to people he doesn't know. Robbie and I went to play on Robbie's computer, and the next thing I know, it was past midnight, and we were still there. I went out to see when we were going home, but my dad said he'd had one too many, and that we were going to stay over, so I slept in Caleb's bed, and my dad ended up sleeping on the couch.

This morning it was totally awkward though, because we didn't have toothbrushes or anything, and my dad was back to being his usual silent self, so we left really early, and didn't have breakfast or anything.

Now my dad is having a nap, and I don't think he'll be going to yoga tonight. I'm going to go to a movie with Robbie. I miss having people to go to the movies with. Christmas is great for movie watching.

Yours truly,
Arthur Bean

▶▶ ▶▶ ▶▶

Merry Christmas!

get anything good?

Some camping stuff. Luke's family gave me this cool screenwriting program. We can write more movies!

ya, cuz that went so well b4

Did you get anything good?

$$$. im gonna save it 4 a car.

when r u back from ur grandmas?

Friday I think. I asked my dad if we could come back early so I could see you. Plus, Balzac is super boring, and Luke leaves tomorrow.

i go home on monday

I thought Calgary was home?

u know what i mean

From: Arthur Bean (arthuraaronbean@gmail.com)
To: Kennedy Laurel (imsocutekl@hotmail.com)
Sent: December 25, 15:04

Dear Kennedy,

I just wanted to wish you a Merry Christmas! I know it's your favourite time of year, and that you love the snow, so you must be loving this year's Christmas season! I was just thinking about our trip to Heritage Park last winter, and how much fun it was! I think that was my favourite part of Christmas last year.

Are you going skiing this year? What are you up to for New Year's Eve?

Yours truly,
Arthur Bean

▶▶ ▶▶ ▶▶

From: Kennedy Laurel (imsocutekl@hotmail.com)
To: Arthur Bean (arthuraaronbean@gmail.com)
Sent: December 26, 13:43

Hi Arthur!

Thanks for your Christmas email! It's been a CRAZY break!

   I was thinking that our first newspaper after the break, we should do an article on resolutions! We can interview students and teachers about their new year's plans! Catie was telling me that her plan was to become a "social tutor"! She claims that she wants to help nerds become more popular! LOL! Can you see Catie helping ANYONE?!?! LOL!! No offence to her, but that is SO not her thing!

Kennedy ☺

From: Von Ipo (thenexteastwood@hotmail.com)
To: Arthur Bean (arthuraaronbean@gmail.com)
Sent: December 26, 15:32

Hey, Arthur!

Merry Christmas buddy! Hope you got some great stuff. My parents got me this sweet new mountain bike. I'm really into mountain biking right now. I was basically shredding the mountain every day this past summer and I rode my bike until it was basically falling apart. So now I have the best bike out there. Can't wait until spring! Do you ride? I bet you'd love it. You can have my old bike if you want. It's basically a beginner bike, but it's still really expensive and pretty great.

Don't know if you're in town, but Rob and I are going to a movie tomorrow. Thought you should come. Like old times last year, all three of us in the AV Club!

Let me know!

Von

Are you seriously going to hang out with Von?

ya

Why?

he asked me 2

Well, good luck with that. He's still as annoying as ever. Maybe more.

never really botherred me

u kno, if u werent so snobby u could have more friends

Dude, I have plenty of friends.

ya, ok. and since were lying now, here comes my new girlfriend selena gomez! gotta go!

▶▶ ▶▶ ▶▶

December 27th

Dear RJ,

Well, I'm glad that's done. What is it about Christmas that makes it so crappy? I know that part of it is that my mom isn't here, and she was so into Christmas, and I miss her a lot, but it's not just that. I even try and get into the Christmas spirit, and I pretend to be happy about it, but I'm really not.

Maybe I'm too old for Christmas. I want to be super excited, but there's never anything really fun to do after we've opened presents. All I got was some camping gear from my dad, a sweater and a book from my grandparents and a computer program. The camping gear is cool, but I can't use it for another six months. I've already read the book, so I have to return it. Everyone just sat around Grandma's living room all afternoon watching a movie. I wanted to go do something else, but because it was Christmas, it feels like we're supposed to spend all day together. Grandpa suggested cross-country skiing, but I'm pretty sure I would hate that, and we didn't have equipment anyway.

It's like Christmas is this big thing that you look forward to for a month, and then it comes and it's just another day, but weirder. There are no toys to play with or be excited about. There's no magic anymore. It's a reminder of the big, gaping hole that my mom left behind, and even watching *Home Alone* can't fix it.

I wonder if other kids feel the same way. I also wonder if Kennedy wrote me back yet. I'm going to go check.

Yours truly,
Arthur Bean

▸▸ ▸▸ ▸▸

December 28th

Dear RJ,

So I get back to Calgary, and Robbie invited Von to join us to hang out tonight! Why would he do that? He knows how much I can't stand that guy! I'm tempted to not even go over there, but Robbie leaves first thing Monday morning, so if I don't go, I'll be sitting at home alone on a Saturday night while my best friend hangs out with my nemesis.

Why does Von have to be everywhere? He's so keen to hang out with me, and I don't know why. I wish he would find other friends. He says he's so popular, so why can't he hang out with those people? And why do only people I don't like want to be my friend?

Yours truly,
Arthur Bean

From: Arthur Bean (arthuraaronbean@gmail.com)
To: Kennedy Laurel (imsocutekl@hotmail.com)
Sent: December 28, 23:00

Dear Kennedy,

Cheesecake Café has a peppermint bark cheesecake!
I saw it when I was there with friends tonight, and I
thought of you. I know you love peppermint bark, and
I remember you said that the Cheesecake Café was
your favourite place. It's like your dream come true!

    I'm sure it'll be around for a little bit longer, so let
me know if you want to go sometime with me and a
bunch of my friends!

Yours truly,
Arthur Bean

▶▶ ▶▶ ▶▶

December 30th

Dear RJ,

The only invitation I got for New Year's Eve
was from Von, and I'm definitely not going to
his hockey team's party. I would rather be by
myself. Although it's going to suck. I'm glad that
I'm not the only one though. Robbie is spending
New Year's with his mom at home.

    Is it wrong that I feel better about myself
because Robbie is doing loser things too? I just
don't want him to have a better time than me. I

think we're better friends if we share the same experiences, even if that means that we both have stupid New Year's plans.

I guess if my social life is at an all-time low, then I want other people's to be also. Do you think this is a sign of what my whole life is going to be like?

Yours truly,
Arthur Bean

JANUARY

Happy New Year!

What terrible movie are you watching tonight? We're watching all the Shrek movies. LAME.

got a last min invite to a movie marathon at dominics! everyone brought a movie. right now were watching the maze runner (doms choice)

and hayleys here! i wanted to kiss her at midnite but i chickened out

Oh. That's great! That sounds fun.

Yeah. mom was really cool about me coming. maybe its her ny resolution to be cooler. ha!

too bad about shrek tho. i hate that donkey. not the best start to the year man.

Well, it can only go up from here!

thats the spirit!

From: Kennedy Laurel (imsocutekl@hotmail.com)
To: Arthur Bean (arthuraaronbean@gmail.com)
Sent: January 1, 16:23

Hi Arthur!

I got your email about the cheesecake, but I was
SO BUSY! Then I forgot to respond, and when I
remembered, it was like December 30th already,
and I figured that I would just talk to you at Rocky's
NYE party, since he invited almost everyone from our
grade. But you weren't there yesterday! It was super
fun! I hope you aren't sick or something. Getting sick
over the holidays is the WORST! ☹

   Anyway, I hope you tried the cheesecake for
me! I can't believe you remembered a stupid little
comment I made about peppermint bark from weeks
ago LOL! But I'm glad you did! Catie and I are
DEFINITELY going to have to try it soon! Thanks for
the heads up!!

Kennedy ☺

From: Arthur Bean (arthuraaronbean@gmail.com)
To: Kennedy Laurel (imsocutekl@hotmail.com)
Sent: January 1, 18:06

Dear Kennedy,

I actually am really sick with the flu. Otherwise, I
would have totally been at the party. I meant to

go, but then I couldn't! It's too bad I missed it. I'll definitely be at the next big party!

I've been thinking about your story about New Year's resolutions, and I have some good ideas. Can I write it? I think I could make it pretty funny!

Yours truly,
Arthur Bean

▶▶ ▶▶ ▶▶

From: Kennedy Laurel (imsocutekl@hotmail.com)
To: Arthur Bean (arthuraaronbean@gmail.com)
Sent: January 3, 20:20

Hi Arthur!

Write away! That's what co-editors are for, right? Sharing ideas and stuff! I've already got some stuff lined up about fundraising for grad (we're doing cookie-grams!!) and about final exams!

Kennedy ☺

▶▶ ▶▶ ▶▶

Assignment: Pickles the Demon Cat

By Arthur Bean

Dear Ms Whitehead,

I'm afraid I can't hand in my homework on time. I know you gave us the whole winter break, but I didn't get it done.

I started to do my homework on the first day of the break, because I am a conscientious student and I like to get everything done early so that I have time to edit and rewrite parts that may need to be fixed. I do this with every assignment, and you never see how much work I put into my writing.

So I started writing, but Pickles, my cat, started meowing. This probably doesn't sound so crazy, but Pickles never makes any noise, so I knew something was wrong. I was certain that this was probably the end for poor Pickles. She's an old cat, and she's clearly annoyed being alive. I don't like her much, but no one should die alone. So I found her, and she was meowing at something outside the window. I looked out, but I couldn't see anything. I opened the window a crack, in case there was gas in the house and she was telling us that we were going to die. Immediately, Pickles jumped through the window and was gone, into the snowstorm that was blowing around outside. I swore (but no one heard me, so it was OK) because I knew that I needed to find Pickles and bring her back inside before she actually died. I grabbed my boots and coat, and ran down the stairs and out the door.

We live on the third floor, which isn't that far for a cat to jump, but I looked under the windowsill first, just in case. No Pickles. I took another step and I heard her meow again. I looked around, and took a step onto the snowy lawn. The snow crackled underneath me, and I fell into a deep hole. I swore again. I was trapped in a deep hole under the snow, and I had no idea what I was going to do! I looked up and saw Pickles smiling at me from above. I know: cats can't smile. But Pickles is part-demon, and she can. And she did. She smiled, and then, the strangest thing happened. She spoke. "Good luck, boy. You'll die in there," she said. I tried to reply, but all that came out of my mouth was a throaty "meow." Pickles cackled and ran off. I was trapped. I looked around and there was no way out. I was stuck. I pulled my coat closer around me. At least it was warm underground.

It was soon dark out, but the snow persisted. Luckily, I had just recently learned about the pukak layer in Mr. Everett's Science class. Since you probably have forgotten what this is, I'll tell you. The pukak layer is a layer of warm air that forms between the ground (or, in this case, me) and the snow falling. It's the reason many animals can stay outside during the winter and not die. I knew that as long as I didn't move, a pukak would form over me and I would be all right. So I huddled in, and sang myself to sleep while the snow fell.

The next thing I knew, it was January 2nd, and a Chinook came through and melted all the snow. I shook myself awake and yawned. I was able to get a foothold in the frozen earth and pull myself out of the hole. When I got to the top, Pickles looked at me with hate in her eyes. "Next time," she said, but the "ime" got stuck in her throat and came out as a purr. I laughed in her face, and said, "Aren't you a good kitty?"

So I barely had time to even write this up, but I hope you accept this as my assignment.

Arthur,

You've crafted an imaginative excuse here. I like your use of knowledge from other classes in your excuse; Mr. Everett would be proud!

I hope that Pickles isn't quite as evil as you say, although maybe that's why I've always been more of a dog person.

Ms Whitehead

▶▶ ▶▶ ▶▶

JOGO: Ban New Year's Resolutions Instead!

By Arthur Bean

January is upon us, which means that people all around the world are pretending that their lives are about to get better, just by saying/writing all the things that they want to change about themselves. Lose ten pounds, read more books, make nerds cooler: these little resolutions hang over people's heads, making the long and cold month of January just that much more disappointing.

Not as disappointing, though, as returning to school to see that a Friday cafeteria favourite, Avril's

Poutine, is off the menu for good.

At first, I thought it was a mistake. Then I thought that maybe someone forgot to order the cheese curds. But no. It was, in fact, a deliberate omission. Ms Kraleigh has taken away our Fry-day.

The Terry Fox Jr. High cafeteria has slowly been shifting towards healthier options, but I know that I was not the only one who appreciated that once a month we were treated to the option of buying crisp, hot fries, salty gravy and squeaky cheese curds. For some students, I'm pretty sure that's the only reason they come to school.

I approached Avril Lonie, the chef in charge of the cafeteria, for a comment, but she shooed me out of the kitchen, claiming that I needed to be wearing a hairnet to be in there. It's possible that this is true, but it's also possible that she has been given a gag order, and is not allowed to speak on the matter.

I don't know why the school administration is trying to suck every bit of enjoyment out of our time here. I don't see why poutine once a month is a bad thing. What is bad is the fact that once a year people make ridiculous claims about trying to become better by setting goals that they will never reach.

Don't ban poutine. Ban New Year's resolutions instead. But hey, that's . . .

Just One Guy's Opinion.

Hey, Arthur,

I know you're against New Year's resolutions, but I don't think they are such a bad thing! Sometimes we need a reminder to do better, the same way that I am, again, reminding you that we cannot skewer the administration for decisions that they make, in each edition of the Marathon. Please edit your piece to make it more diplomatic and objective and re-submit. I know you can do it; we've had lots of practice on your earlier pieces.

Cheers,
Mr. E.

▶▶ ▶▶ ▶▶

From: Kennedy Laurel (imsocutekl@hotmail.com)
To: Arthur Bean (arthuraaronbean@gmail.com)
Sent: January 9, 16:02

ARTHUR!!

I CAN'T believe that THIS is what you meant when you said you wanted to write the New Year's resolutions article!! That isn't at all what I thought you were going to do! I feel like you totally misled me into trusting you with this!
    Why did you write this?! I thought that we were FINALLY getting back to normal after all the stuff from last year, and then you go and break my trust with this?!?

Kennedy ☹

From: Arthur Bean (arthuraaronbean@gmail.com)
To: Kennedy Laurel (imsocutekl@hotmail.com)
Sent: January 9, 17:17

Dear Kennedy,

I wasn't skewering what you wanted to write. I just thought it was a good angle to take when they took poutine off the menu. I really didn't do it to make you angry!

I'm just writing what I think, and what others might be thinking too. That's why my articles are called JOGO!

I want us to be friends, but imagine if everyone always agreed with you? Would you want your boyfriend to always think all the same things as you do? That would be so boring!

The *Marathon* is for debating issues and putting forward points of view for our readers. I promise you, this wasn't a personal attack!!

Yours truly,
Arthur Bean

From: Kennedy Laurel (imsocutekl@hotmail.com)
To: Arthur Bean (arthuraaronbean@gmail.com)
Sent: January 9, 20:15

Let's be clear. You are my co-editor, NOT my boyfriend. We're SUPPOSED to AGREE on what goes in the paper! That's what the *CO* part means in front of *editor*.

January 9th

Dear RJ,

I got called into a meeting with Mr. Everett today, and you'll never believe what he said! He said that Ms Kraleigh has some serious concerns about my work on the newspaper! Even AFTER I changed all the stuff about the administration in my poutine article. I don't get it at all! I'm just trying to provide a counterpoint to some of the decisions that she's making, and she shuts me down! Mr. Everett said that she feels that I'm attacking her personally, and that I am, get this, "undermining her ability to effect positive change." I put this in quotes, because that's what it sounded like when Mr. Everett said it to me. He would never talk like that; he's too dorky. RJ, I'm not the kind of guy to rock the boat, but I think this is kind of crazy! I should be able to say what I want! Even Mr. Everett agreed with me that I back up my opinions with valid arguments. Frankly, I think they should all be proud that I actually learned something from Ms Whitehead and follow her laws about persuasive writing. I was so mad. I asked Mr. Everett if I was getting kicked off the paper, and he assured me that I wasn't, but that we would have to tread carefully with this new administration. I felt kind of bad for him, being caught in the middle. I think he's mad about it too, but he never said that. He said that both Ms Kraleigh and I had valid points, but that she was in charge here, not me.

Now I don't know what I'm going to write about for the next edition of the *Marathon*. Everybody's jumping down my throat for such little things!

I was going to write about changing the school mascot to something more original than a fox, but I kind of want to write about free speech instead. I should write about how my basic rights as a citizen are being taken away! I should write about the Charter of Rights and Freedoms! I could be the next Braveheart!! FREEDOM!!

Yours truly,
Arthur Bean

▶▶ ▶▶ ▶▶

From: Von Ipo (thenexteastwood@hotmail.com)
To: Arthur Bean (arthuraaronbean@gmail.com)
Sent: January 11, 9:32

Hey, Artie!

Great rehearsal yesterday, hey? Loved how funny everyone is! I toned down what I was going to do, because I wanted to make sure that everyone got a chance to be funny, otherwise I would basically steal the show. Isn't it awesome to have your words spoken by other people?

Also, Millie is super hot! Think you could give me her number? I'm surprised I don't have it already — I basically have everyone's number in our grade. I want to invite her to my hockey game tomorrow. Actually, now that I think of it, you guys could come together! I'll invite her and then we could all hang out after. You could basically be my wingman!

Von

Von wants me to be his wingman. Ha!
Like I would help that guy get a date!

why not? he would help u

Seriously, Robbie. He's annoying.
He thinks he's so much better than
everyone else. Plus he wants me to set
him up with Millie. And I'm pretty sure
she's in love with me.

Ha! pot=kettle=black

I don't think I'm better than everyone!
I just know that Millie would definitely
NOT be interested in Von.

well let him down easy

From: Arthur Bean (arthuraaronbean@gmail.com)
To: Von Ipo (thenexteastwood@hotmail.com)
Sent: January 11, 20:41

Von,

I don't have Millie's number, so I can't give it to you.
I just see her at fencing. She fences a lot though, so I
don't think she has time for a boyfriend anyway.
See you Monday.

Arthur Bean

January 16th

Dear RJ,

I found out during fencing today that Millie is super in love with Vincent. I was sure she was into me! I'm kind of glad that she's not, but it's also kind of confusing. I was sure she was flirting with me. I don't think I was supposed to find out about her liking Vincent anyway, but she and Joie were talking about it and I couldn't help but overhear. No one else at fencing really pays attention to me, so I spend a lot of time feeling like a lurker around Joie and Millie and waiting for them to acknowledge me so I can join in the conversation. At least they always do acknowledge me. It's better than some girls I know.

I'm not allowed to tell anyone her secret, because Vincent doesn't know, which is weird. I told her to tell him, but she said that she could never do that because she's not his type. How does she know? If she's never really talked to him, how does she know she's not his type? Plus, people date surprising people all the time. Like how Kennedy and I were together. I bet a bunch of people probably never thought that would happen! I told Millie this, but then she said that she had heard that Kennedy and I never really were together. Which kind of proved my point that the rumour mill is never right. But man, am I glad that she doesn't like Von! Ha!

Anyway, I'm thinking now that maybe it's Joie who likes me, and Millie was just trying to make it seem like it was her. Not that I would date Joie. She's nice, but she's a way better fencer than me, and she's super competitive.

Yours truly,
Arthur Bean

▶▶ ▶▶ ▶▶

i sent in my app for summer camp

Aren't you too old to go back? I thought you had to be 14 and under.

ya i know. im gonna be a counsilor

Ha! Not with spelling like that, you won't.

just watch me

▶▶ ▶▶ ▶▶

Assignment: Book Review Two

The Absolutely True Diary of a Part-Time Indian
by Sherman Alexie

I read this book because the librarian told me it was really good. And boy, was she right! It's a pretty great book, and I particularly liked that it's been banned in so many places. I am particularly drawn to books that have been banned these days. I like to push the envelope. For example, did you know that Harry Potter has been banned? I don't understand some people. What's so terrible about wizards?

Anyway, this book had everything you would want in a book. A hilarious protagonist, a complicated history and some touching moments. If I ever write a book, I hope that it's as good as this book. In fact, this is the kind of book where I read it, and I told my dad to read it, because I wish that I had written the book. Some books are so good that I can't help but be jealous that I didn't write them myself. Also, I liked that it had doodles in it, but I'm a pretty bad illustrator, so I would get Robbie to do that part for me.

The one thing is that I'm glad that this wasn't my life, because I've had some pretty terrible things happen to me so far, but nothing as bad as Junior's life. Overall, I give it five stars out of five stars.

Arthur,

The Absolutely True Diary of a Part-Time Indian is not a real biography. I'll agree with you that it's an excellent book, but it does not fit into the parameters of the original reading assignment. Please choose a different biography to review. I'll accept this piece as an extra-credit assignment so that you receive credit for your work here.

Ms Whitehead

Dear Ms Whitehead,

I think we need to agree to disagree. The title clearly states that it's a true story, and I read a lot about the author, and he's First Nations. He may have partially fictionalized his life for the book, but I still think it should count, because: a) it was a really awesome book and everyone should read it, b) it's not a fantasy novel and c) the only other biographies that I found that sounded interesting were all about old comedians. Reading this book opens my horizons way more than knowing where Steve Martin did his first stand-up comedy routine, don't you think?

Yours truly,
Arthur Bean

Arthur,

You do weave a compelling argument. Let's compromise: come by my classroom and we can discuss The Absolutely True Diary of a Part-Time Indian in depth. I'll provide you with the discussion questions ahead of time so that you can prepare thoughtful responses for our conversation.

Ms Whitehead

▶▶ ▶▶ ▶▶

January 21st

Dear RJ,

I could actually start to like this fencing thing. Millie and Joie's class is super fun, mostly because they are there, but also we get to fence more! The only part that sucks is that we had to do wind sprints to warm up, which I tried to get out of, and then Deeter made me do more than everyone else, which made me really mad. But after that, we did some practice moves where I learned a new attack move, and then we actually got to hook up to the electric machines and score our bouts. We never got to do that in the lame beginner course. If we had done that on the first day, it would have been way better. Every fencer is hooked up to an electric wire that runs down the inside of your jacket, and it hooks up to the machine. Then you have this metal jacket called a lamé, and if you hit your opponent's lamé, the coloured light goes on. If you hit them on the sleeve or whatever, the white light goes on. Sometimes all the lights go on at once, and that's when the ref has to decide who hit whom first. It was so cool. I barely made any coloured lights go on, but I fenced against Joie and I got the first point. Then she got mad and beat me in like 10 seconds, but still. I got the first point! I watched Millie and Joie fight each other. It was so fast paced. They are really good!

I think Dad was glad that he didn't have to go, but he did seem a bit sad about it when I told him that it was way cooler this semester. I asked him if he wanted to rejoin, but he said he was going to stick to something more passive. It's probably for the best. To be honest, RJ, I didn't really want him to come back anyway.

Yours truly,
Arthur Bean

▸▸ ▸▸ ▸▸

Can you make me some scenery for my play?

can u pay me?

No.

ok ill do it

wat do u need?

It's about spies, and it takes place in a secret spy room. I wanted some cool portraits on the walls of famous spies.

like this?

EXACTLY

▶▶ ▶▶ ▶▶

January 30th

Dear RJ,

Rehearsal was good today. Von was less
annoying, but I think that's because he has
strep throat so he's not allowed to talk very
much. I watched a couple of other rehearsals
too while I was waiting for Dad to pick me up,
and my play is definitely going to be the best.
I just kind of wish I could be in my own play!
Hark says that we need to learn how to work
with others as directors, and that it's good to
hear our words in other voices. He's probably
right, even though I have to remind myself of
this every time Von says his lines wrong and I
have to correct him. I tried to tell him exactly
how to say the lines to make them funny, but he
never does the same voice as I do.

In other good news, Kennedy seems to
have forgiven me for the New Year's resolution
article. She was being super fun and hilarious
in today's newspaper meeting. She even
touched my shoulder at one point when she
was laughing about something I said. So that's
definitely a step in the right direction. I think
maybe she is waiting for me to extend an olive
branch so that we can be real friends again.

Yours truly,
Arthur Bean

FEBRUARY

From: Arthur Bean (arthuraaronbean@gmail.com)
To: Kennedy Laurel (imsocutekl@hotmail.com)
Sent: February 2, 9:30

Dear Kennedy,

Happy Groundhog Day!
   I don't know if you're busy, but I was thinking of watching this movie called *Groundhog Day* today. It's really old, but it's really funny. I know you love funny movies, and I bet you haven't seen this one! Let me know if you want to come over. I'm home all day, so whenever works for you. It'll be like old times!

Yours truly,
Arthur Bean

From: Kennedy Laurel (imsocutekl@hotmail.com)
To: Arthur Bean (arthuraaronbean@gmail.com)
Sent: February 2, 17:17

Hi Arthur,

I actually hate Bill Murray! I can't believe that people like him! I don't think he's funny at all! He just smirks all the time! My brother made me watch a bunch of his movies a couple of years ago and I've made sure to NEVER watch another one LOL!

But I really hope you enjoy your movie!!

Kennedy ☺

February 2nd

Dear RJ,

I really wanted someone to watch *Groundhog Day* with me today, but there was no one around. I tried a bunch of people. I got so desperate that I even considered calling Von, but c'mon, RJ, I'm not a sucker for torture! I don't have Millie or Joie's phone numbers, but even if I did, I don't know if I would have called them. RJ, I don't know how to make friends. Like, how do I invite them over without it sounding like a date? And what if they laugh at me and say no?

Anyway, in the end, the three people I asked were busy, so now I'm just waiting for Dad to get home. I know he'll watch it with me. He loves Bill Murray. But still, I'm a guy whose only plans this weekend were watching a movie with his dad.

Yours truly,
Arthur Bean

⏩ ⏩ ⏩

I won a bout tonight!

that makes no sense. about what?

A fencing match, idiot. A bout.

no doubt A BOUT it!

You're the biggest dork of all time.

im not the 1 who swordfights 4 a living

▶▶ ▶▶ ▶▶

February 7th

Dear RJ,

You won't believe it; I am SO MAD at Kraleigh.

We were rehearsing this afternoon after school, and we were just coming to the big climax scene when she walked into the Drama room. She stood in the doorway, leaning on it, listening. I didn't really want her to see my play, but I also thought she should see that I am a great director and a great writer, so we kept going. But after we were done, she walked all the way in and demanded to speak to Hark. He was in the other room, helping Georgia and Simon develop their romance play. (It's so boring right now. It's basically them making out and telling each other that they love each other, the same way they do at the back of homeroom every morning.) ANYWAY, Kraleigh stormed in there and pulled Hark out into the hall. They were out there for a long time, but eventually only Hark came back in and said that we had to put a pause on rehearsals for the time being.

You know why?!? She thought my play was too violent!!!

Hark told us that she was questioning some of the content in our plays, and that she wanted to read them over before they were performed publically. And she only saw mine, so she clearly hates me and wants to ruin my life. I can't think of anything other than the fact that some guy dies that would be questionable. And it's not questionable; it's funny!!

I wanted to yell at her, but Kraleigh had already left, and Hark was trying so hard to stay calm about it. I wanted to scream, but I know it's not Hark's fault that she's so awful.

I can't believe that she would stoop to this level. She should be more professional! I'm pretty sure it's against the law for teachers to have personal vendettas against students. I wonder if there's someone I could complain to, maybe the head of the school board or something. This is totally unfair. We've been working on these plays for so long! Not only that, but Hark already okayed all the plays. He's the Drama teacher, not Kraleigh. He should get the final say!

Yours truly,
Arthur Bean

From: Von Ipo (thenexteastwood@hotmail.com)
To: Arthur Bean (arthuraaronbean@gmail.com)
Sent: February 8, 11:07

Hey, Arthur!

Bummer about yesterday, hey? I hope we get to start up again soon! You seemed really mad, which I get. But I guess she's kind of got a point. The school basically has a no-gun policy, so it probably counts for the theatre department too. But still, what a crappy thing to have happen.

I was thinking that if we can't do our plays as plays, you and I could make them into movies! Bet Hark would let us do that if we asked. Especially if you're involved. I think you're like his fave student!

Von

> The new principal definitely hates me!

ya we new that

wat did she do this time?

> She basically cancelled our play festival because of my play!

it was that bad?

132

NO. It was that good.

so . . . no play festival?

She's reading all the plays to decide if we can do them. She's a dictator!

u should quit and move to lethbridge. my school is pretty chill

But then I would have to see your face every day.

more like u would have 2 live with caleb and my mom.

Yeah, that's not going to happen.

▶▶ ▶▶ ▶▶

Assignment: Superstitions

We're starting *Macbeth* this week! I think you'll enjoy the elements of the supernatural, the bloody battles and treasonous acts found in this Shakespearean tragedy. We're going to take our time reading this play, and studying different aspects of Shakespeare, and the unit will culminate with a field trip; we'll get the chance to see *Macbeth* at Theatre Calgary later this year!

A main theme in *Macbeth* is one of superstition. In fact, in the acting community, saying the word "Macbeth" is considered unlucky, so you'll often hear it referred to as "The Scottish Play." Write a one-page reflective essay on superstitions. What are some superstitions that you have heard about? Provide examples of superstitions people you know believe. Do *you* believe in superstitions? Why or why not?

Due: February 17

February 11th

Dear RJ,

I stopped in to talk to Hark today at lunch and see what was happening with our Leg Breakers plays. He seemed so stressed out! He said that we would just have to wait and see. He felt so bad that this was happening. He said that he should have known better and that he screwed up because he told us to push the envelope with our pieces. But that's not true, and I told him so! He's been the best teacher I've ever had, and I think that he's awesome. He smiled and thanked me for saying so, but said that we would see what the future holds, and that, even if we couldn't do our plays, we would find something equally great to do.

But I'm going to do my play. We're going to make it happen, even if it's without Hark. I don't plan to be stopped by just a lowly principal!

Yours truly,
Arthur Bean

▶▶ ▶▶ ▶▶

i got a date for valentines day!

Yeah right. Who would go out with you?

hayley would

Yeah right.

no its true i asked her if she was dating dominic and she said def not. then she asked if i wanted to go w them 4 pizza friday nite.

That's not a date, Robbie.

well it is after i asked her if dominic had 2 come, or if maybe it could be just her + i

And she laughed in your face.

AND SHE SAID YES

SO WHAT R U DOING?! A date with ur cat?? HAHAHAHAHA

▶▶ ▶▶ ▶▶

February 14th

Dear RJ,

So it's Valentine's Day, so what? It's just another normal day. There's nothing that I'm missing out on today by not having a girlfriend. In fact, I'm not even interested in any girls. I don't care what Kennedy and whoever she's dating these days are doing tonight. Whatever it is, I'm sure it's lame. I'm pretty convinced that no one actually likes romance. It's so much work, and it feels so fake. Besides, what is romantic about winter in Calgary? It's freezing cold and covered in snow. Yeah, like that's a good time to strike up a romance. Ha! I'm glad I'm not dating anyone! I can just hang out and do whatever I want tonight. Everyone else is a sucker!

Yours truly,
Arthur Bean

▶▶ ▶▶ ▶▶

Yeah? So???

Are you jelous??

I'm not jealous. I'm just really busy right now.

ya rite. dont you want to hear about my awesome night?

Not really, but I think you really want to brag, so you can call me and I'll put the phone down while you ramble on.

CALLING NOW

February 15th

Dear RJ,

Robbie kissed Hayley last night. I don't know how that guy learned such smooth moves. He sure never had charm like that last year. Maybe there's something in the wind in Lethbridge. I bet the wind just gusted and he lost his balance and his face fell onto her lips.

It's not fair, RJ. Why does he get a girlfriend, and I can't even get a friend? His brother is a criminal and he's bad at spelling and his mom is super strict! I'm a good-looking, really smart and funny guy with a heart of gold. In the movies my mom used to watch, it's me who's supposed to get the girl, not guys like Robbie.

I don't mean it, RJ. I know Robbie's cool and stuff. I know I should be happy that his life is turning out perfect. But I can't help feeling annoyed. Why does nothing like that ever work out for me?

Yours truly,
Arthur Bean

▶▶ ▶▶ ▶▶

Assignment: Superstitions

By Arthur Bean

One can't help but be superstitious when you need all the help in life that you can get. Which is probably why so many people believe in superstitions.

I wish I could tell you that I'm above all that and I think they're dumb, but I think a lot of superstitions became superstitions because they are actually just good advice. Take, for example, "Never walk under a ladder." Of course you shouldn't walk under a ladder! The person using the ladder could fall on top of you! They won't die, but you sure could. So, I follow "Never walk under the ladder" as part of the Laws of A. Bean.

Another superstition that is one of the Laws of A. Bean is "You will have bad luck if a black cat crosses your path." This one is particularly true. Pickles is a black-and-white cat and seriously, every second time she walks in front of me, something bad happens that day. She walked in front of me yesterday: BAM! Surprise Science quiz! A few weeks ago, she walked in front of me twice in one day, and I stubbed my toe on the couch and burnt my tongue on dinner. Clearly, there is some kind of evil force at work here.

One superstition that I really like, but have yet to put to the test, is that you can never give someone a knife as a gift, or else it will sever your relationship. I'm considering trying it with someone . . . maybe, I don't know, Ms Kraleigh. You know, just to test it out. If she goes away and we never see each other again, then I'll put it on my list!

There are a few that don't make any sense to me. For example, there's one about red skies and sailors that my mom used to say, but I am highly sceptical that it matters to sailors what colour the skies are in Alberta. There's a mountain range between us and the next ocean. If they are worried about that, they have bigger problems, namely, the fact that they should be able to avoid a mountain range in their boat, so maybe they should consider a career change.

The one that makes me really roll my eyes is that you should never light three cigarettes with the same match. You know why? Because you shouldn't be lighting cigarettes in the first place. They're gross and they stink, and of course you're going to die if you smoke. Maybe this superstition is there to stop dumbasses who smoke from having friends who smoke too. I guess there's a reason for everything.

Arthur,

First, please watch your language in your assignments. It's not appropriate, even if I might agree with you about the detriments of smoking.

Second, while I appreciate the sentiments that you've laid out in describing which superstitions you believe in versus which you do not, I would like you to work on developing a professional tone to your work. Your narrative voice is quite casual, and while it works for some pieces, it's important that you are able to pull yourself away from the subject matter and write in a more neutral manner.

Ms Whitehead

▶▶ ▶▶ ▶▶

hayley told the whole school that im her boyfriend

Is that good? It sounds bad.

no its good! now a bunch of other hot girls r being super nice 2 me

But why would that matter? You're with Hayley.

i know but i got invited to 3 different parties this w-end! im like the coolest guy at school!

There are three parties on the same weekend? Are there enough people in Lethbridge for that?

dude, theres lots of people here. and there pretty cool

Are you sure you're not just saying that because you live there now and you've been brainwashed?

your being pretty judgmental 4 a guy whose never been here

Well, maybe you should invite me to come and visit!

the invite is open man. come this weekend!

I can't this weekend. I've got a huge Social report to do. Sorry.

no prob. maybe another time

▶▶ ▶▶ ▶▶

Dear Leg Breakers,

I wanted to apologize to all of you for the miscommunication that led to this afternoon's meeting. I know you all worked very hard on your plays, and I'm so proud of all the blood, sweat and tears that you put into writing them. They are all fantastic, and you should be so happy with them!

As you heard from Ms Kraleigh today, the content that we tackled in our plays isn't really appropriate for a public play festival. I should have consulted with her before we went forward as far as we did.

This doesn't mean the end of the Leg Breakers, though! We still have time to mount a play, and Ms Kraleigh has suggested something that could be great. We'll be performing Coming of Age, a musical all about being a teenager! I remember my school put it on when I was in junior high, and with a little updating, I think we can really make it shine!

If any of you would like to talk about this more, my classroom door is always open. Let's look at this as a learning opportunity for all of us, and a chance to tackle a different type of challenge!

Love you guys for being so cool about all this!

Hark

February 24th

Dear RJ,

I was so mad about today's Leg Breakers meeting
that I almost didn't go to fencing. Dad told me
that I'd probably feel better hitting something,
so I went, and he was right. At least I got to
forget about it for a few minutes. But then Millie
brought it up, and then I got mad again.

I can't believe that Kraleigh would do this!
It's not like we're six years old. We're practically
adults! I'm sure it was my play that she hated,
because she has no sense of humour, and even
though she acted like she was talking about all
our plays, I could tell that she wanted to just be
talking to me.

We've been working so hard on these shows.
We should be allowed to show our plays,
especially since people would be paying to see
them. They are choosing to come; if the subject
matter insults them, then they could just not
come! This is definitely not over, RJ. I'm not
going to just let her do whatever she wants!

Yours truly,
Arthur Bean

▶▶ ▶▶ ▶▶

February 28th

Dear RJ,

We read through *Coming of Age* today, and
there's NO way I'm doing that play for Leg
Breakers. It's the worst play ever written. We
had a read-through today after school and
it was awful. It was written in the 80s, and
it's so stupid. The songs are titled things like
"Peer Pressure, You're Bringing Me Down," and
"Puberty Blues!" The plot is really lame, and
the whole thing is embarrassing to read, so I
can't imagine what it would be like to act. Hark
pretended like it was really great, but when
the whole group was groaning about it, he said
that it wasn't so bad, and we could work as a
team to fix it and make it more contemporary.
But I think it's unfixable. I definitely won't be
in it, and I told Hark that. I felt bad telling him,
especially because a bunch of other people in
the group said that they didn't want to do it
either. I know he's just trying to make us feel
better, but I don't know why he doesn't just tell
Kraleigh to back off and let us do our own thing.

Yours truly,
Arthur Bean

MARCH

Assignment: Design a Set

Imagine yourself as a set designer for *Macbeth*. Draw a set design for one scene that we have already studied (you may choose any scene up to act 3, scene 1). Along with your set-design drawing, include a short paragraph explaining some of the decisions you have made to bring the play to life. Remember that sets can be designed to show symbols or bring out characterization as well!

Due: March 14

March 6th

Dear RJ,

I talked to Millie and Ben (and Von too, but he doesn't really count) about the Leg Breakers, and we have a plan. I'm going to write an article for the *Marathon* about the recent controversy! I think that maybe we can get more people on our side when they hear about how we aren't allowed to do our plays. Like Millie said, it's a question of free speech! We should be allowed to do them!

I know that I've already gotten in trouble for articles in the *Marathon*, so I'll have to be super careful to be objective, but I think that I can pull it off.

Ben suggested that we get the other Leg

Breakers on board, keep rehearsing and perform the plays anyway. He said we could probably get away with it, because Kraleigh can't stop us if she doesn't know that we're going to perform them!

I'm pumped, RJ. It feels so awesome being surrounded by people who are as mad as I am. And every famous person has a story of rebelling against authority. Plus, the best books and plays have been banned at some point too. The way I see it, my play could be the next Harry Potter phenomenon! If it's edgy, we might even get MORE people coming to our festival!

Yours truly,
Arthur Bean

▶▶ ▶▶ ▶▶

I'm staging a coup!

i think youve flown the coup. what r u talkin about?

A coup! We're going to put our plays on even though Kraleigh doesn't want us to!

wow such a rebell

I know! Ben and Millie and Von are helping me.

good luck!

oh ya and i got an interview at camp!

An interview? For what?

a councilor job, i have 2 go over brake

So you'll be here for spring break?

part of it. hayley doesnt want me gone the whole time

Awesome. We can hang out while you're here!

▶▶ ▶▶ ▶▶

March 10th

Dear RJ,

I'm going to enter a fencing competition! It's not until June, but Deeter said that he thinks I'll be ready and that I have a great chance to do pretty well if I focus and practise a lot. Millie said that she would practise with me on the weekends if she's around (her and Joie go to a lot of competitions, so they aren't here that often), and she said that Joie would come too. Joie actually owns two swords, and Deeter said that we could maybe borrow equipment if we're really careful. I just hope that Joie doesn't want to do footwork drills all the time. Those are the worst.

The competition is a pretty big deal; it's the Calgary regionals. If you win this one, you could even go to provincials, which are being held in Lethbridge in the fall! So if I win, I would even get to visit Robbie. Although maybe he'll move back for high school. If I were him, I would. I think he really hates Lethbridge.

I wonder what Kennedy would say if she knew that I was now a competitive fencer. That's way cooler than being an athlete on some dumb school volleyball team!

Yours truly,
Arthur Bean

▸▸ ▸▸ ▸▸

Can you send me a couple of drawings of ghosts? Little ones?

what kind of ghosts?

Scary ones. And a king. And a witch.

Make that three witches.

what is this 4?

I'm working on a set design.

here they are!

Dude, I mean actually scary. Not "scary if you're four."

rite. like u werent scarred by casper

I take it you were?

dude that guy was terrifying!!! he talked so much and had a creepy laugh

this better?

Definitely. Thanks. This takes my homework to a whole new level!

homework? does this mean u will do my essay?

It's not the whole thing. Just the decoration. And I'll give you credit!

then u have to help me w my essay over the brake

Deal! I can't wait until you're here!

▶▶ ▶▶ ▶▶

Assignment: Set Design

By Arthur Bean

I have designed Macbeth's bedroom where
he meets Lady Macbeth after killing the king.
I made sure that there were things to sit on,
because I know that you need many different
levels when you're directing a play, and people
need to be able to sit and stand in different
places, especially in a Shakespeare play when it's
all talking and no action. There's a bed, because
it's a bedroom, and I pictured Macbeth lying
down after the strain of killing someone. I think
that would take a lot out of a person.

I added an extra level with stairs; people love
stairs onstage. It looks so fancy. Plus, this way
they can wheel the bed out and change things
up downstairs, and make it into different parts
of the castle easily.

I wanted to add an extra level of symbolism to the walls, so I added in a painting of a ghost (foreshadowing), three witches (backshadowing) and the king (RIP). The painting would be an original, and so to show that, I have asked an artist to draw that part of my set for me.

Arthur,

Your set design is well done, if not a little basic. You have all the elements that are needed, but nothing more. I was hoping that you would have been more creative with your design, but I like the addition of Robbie's doodle. Next time, assume that your theatre company is in New York, has a huge budget for set design, and dream bigger!

Ms Whitehead

▶▶ ▶▶ ▶▶

JOGO: Age-Appropriate Material

By Arthur Bean

Terry Fox Jr. High has never had any major problems. In general, we're pretty good kids. Nobody has killed anyone else over an ex-boyfriend; nobody has even died of an accidental peanuting from a lethal allergy. As far as I know, no one has even come close to dying here. So it may come as a surprise to many of you that the upcoming Leg Breakers play festival has been cancelled due to the material that was going to be presented.

I see this having a number of problems. First, it's being cancelled because the administration feels that the audience can't handle what we've written about. But the audience will be our families and friends and other kids in our school. These are all people we see on a daily basis. They know us. And I bet they are smart too. I bet they understand that even though the actor may pretend to shoplift something, they aren't actually shoplifting. I bet they understand that just because someone gets shot onstage, they aren't actually dead. I'm certain that they know that the guns aren't real, but are props. I think we need to give our audience some credit.

Secondly, why can't we do whatever we want? Shouldn't we be able to write about difficult subjects? We're taught to think about issues and debate them in class, but suddenly when we put them onstage, it's not appropriate? That's just plain weird. I don't think that there should be rules that tell us what we can and cannot say in our plays. It's a question of freedom of speech. Aren't we allowed it?

So instead of banning us from doing our plays, I think we should just put a warning on the program that "Some material may be shocking to some viewers." But hey, that's . . .

Just One Guy's Opinion.

Hey, Artie,

Can you stop by my classroom later today? I want to chat with you about your most recent article.

Cheers!
Mr. E.

March 20th

Dear RJ,

We have an ally! Mr. Everett met with me today and said that he agreed with my article, and that we might need to make a few adjustments, but that we can print it in the *Marathon*. He said that I expressed my opinion fairly and politely, but that we'll look at making sure that there's nothing that can be read "with attitude." (Ha! Like I have attitude! I prefer to call it "personality.") We're going to publish it in tomorrow's paper, so that when we get back from spring break, Kraleigh will have had ten days to change her mind. I knew there were teachers on our side! I bet we could even get some more teachers to support us if we needed to. There's no way Ms Whitehead would be pro-censorship of my work; she's a fan of my work. And Mr. E. seems pretty popular; I bet he could get the teachers to go on strike for us if they had to! I think that having Hark and Mr. E. on our side, we can show Kraleigh who's really in charge!

Yours truly,
Arthur Bean

▶▶ ▶▶ ▶▶

From: Kennedy Laurel (imsocutekl@hotmail.com)
To: Arthur Bean (arthuraaronbean@gmail.com)
Sent: March 21, 16:50

Hi Arthur!

Wow! Your article this week is pretty heavy! I had no idea that this was going on! I feel bad! I've been really busy with grad stuff and all kinds of other stupid things! (Catie and I got into a HUGE fight last week, but things are better now LOL!) ANYWAY, I'm totally behind you on this! Good luck! (Wait, isn't it bad luck to wish someone good luck in the theatre LOL?!)

Kennedy ☺

From: Arthur Bean (arthuraaronbean@gmail.com)
To: Kennedy Laurel (imsocutekl@hotmail.com)
Sent: March 21, 18:37

Dear Kennedy,

Thanks! Your support means a lot to me. We've been fighting this for a long time, but I've got a good team behind me. I'm positive that I can make Kraleigh change her mind. If you want to help us, you could join the Leg Breakers! If you joined us, we would be even stronger!

Yours truly,
Arthur Bean

From: Kennedy Laurel (imsocutekl@hotmail.com)
To: Arthur Bean (arthuraaronbean@gmail.com)
Sent: March 21, 19:56

Hi Arthur!

I'm so, SO busy that I can't join you guys. But I'm sure it'll be great, no matter what!

Kennedy ☺

i have arrived

You're in Calgary?

here for 4 days

Great! I'm leaving on Thursday for Edmonton to hang out with Luke.

im free everyday, xcept that i have to call hayley @ 6

At 6 today? Didn't you just leave Lethbridge?

no 6 everyday. we agreed

What if you're busy?

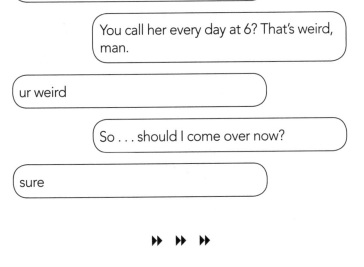

no u dont get it. i HAVE to call at 6. its a thing we do

You call her every day at 6? That's weird, man.

ur weird

So . . . should I come over now?

sure

From: Von Ipo (thenexteastwood@hotmail.com)
To: Arthur Bean (arthuraaronbean@gmail.com)
Sent: March 24, 20:41

Hey, Arthur!

Ben's having a party on Friday night and he asked me if I could help him spread the word. He knows that I'm basically friends with everyone, I guess! Anyway, you should come. I know Kennedy and Catie are definitely going. Piper is going to come, and Lucia and Mai and Latha too. I invited Mackenzie and her older sister, and Lili and Yoshie. I think some guys are coming too.

My mom could pick you up if you want to go together!

See you Friday!

Von

i think im gonna stay and go 2 bens party fri

What? Why? You hate most of the people going.

ya but i like ben and von will b there. and i can avoid everyone i dont like

I can't go, though. I'm going to see Luke, and I already have my bus ticket.

What about Hayley? I thought you were going back to see her.

she will still be there on sat. its not like were married

Don't go to the party. Come to Edmonton with me! Luke won't mind.

i dont know luke. why would i do that?

To hang out with me? Because I'm awesome?

haha. u wish

I bet the party will suck anyway.

well ill let u know!

▶▶ ▶▶ ▶▶

March 26th

Dear RJ,

This sucks. I've never not wanted to go hang
out with Luke before! I always want to hang out
with Luke. But now there's this party in town,
and Robbie's even going, and I don't want to
miss it. I feel like I will be a super nerd if I miss
it, and people will think that I didn't get invited,
but really, I just can't go. I asked my dad if I
could go to Edmonton on Saturday instead of
tomorrow, but he said that Auntie Deborah
has something planned for us on Friday, and
that you don't just change plans on someone
because you got a better offer. I can't even
pretend that I'm sick now, because my dad will
know that I'm just trying to get out of going.
I want to call and ask Luke if he'd be mad if I
didn't come, but I don't want him to feel like I
don't want to hang out.

    It figures. I'm finally invited to a party, and I
can't even go.

Yours truly,
Arthur Bean

From: Arthur Bean (arthuraaronbean@gmail.com)
To: Von Ipo (thenexteastwood@hotmail.com)
Sent: March 26, 11:21

Dear Von,

Thanks for letting me know about Ben's party. I wish I could go, but I'm going out of town this weekend. I'll probably go to some pretty big parties in Edmonton, but I feel bad that I can't go to Ben's. I hope that not everybody at school is away this weekend. That would suck if no one can go, but then maybe he would do it on another day.

Arthur Bean

From: Von Ipo (thenexteastwood@hotmail.com)
To: Arthur Bean (arthuraaronbean@gmail.com)
Sent: March 26, 13:40

Dude, it's too bad that you can't come. Basically everybody is coming! I think you're like the only lucky guy who's going away for spring break this year. Also made sure that Millie is coming. I'm going to make my move!! She told Ben she's bringing a friend too. So if Millie isn't into me, maybe her friend will be!

Have a good time in Edmonton. Let's hang when you're back!

Von

▶▶ ▶▶ ▶▶

How was the party? Did I miss anything?

u missed alot of ppl making out

Like who?

how do i know? i dont live here

Did you stay long?

long enough

Did you see Kennedy there?

ya she was there, but was busy

Busy? Like making out with someone busy? With who?

dude i ignorred her

Did Von hit on Millie?

i dont know millie. maybe?

Millie has bright red hair. She would have been there with another girl with super-long hair named Joie. Were they there?

the girls hair is named joie??

You know what I mean!

i dont know. u allways correct my grammar. u should be more careful in planning your texts.

Were Millie and Joie there?

dude I DONT KNOW

Are you leaving today?

im already on the bus. should i wave as i leave the city?

Don't bother.

dont cry, artie. im back at easter

APRIL

April 1st

Dear RJ,

Kraleigh was so mad about my article that she
actually came to our Leg Breakers meeting. She
said that she had made a decision about our
plays, and that we should be mature enough
to understand that the school administration
makes decisions based on protecting children.
She talked to us like we were five years old. So I
told her straight up that we disagreed with her
decision, and everyone cheered for me. It felt
amazing. Now I know what it will feel like when
I win an Oscar. It was like being on top of the
world when I stood up to her.

I only felt bad after, when Hark looked like
he wanted to crawl under a rock and disappear.
I guess he's kind of stuck in the middle. I know
he wants to help us out, but he can't because
the principal is his boss. I wonder if there's a
way to make him feel better and still do our
plays.

Yours truly,
Arthur Bean

▶▶ ▶▶ ▶▶

Assignment: *Macbeth* scenes

Now that we've finished reading *Macbeth*, it's time to bring it to life! Choose a group of one to four students, and create a commercial for something inspired by our reading of *Macbeth*. It could be something that a character could use (maybe a spot remover for Lady Macbeth), or a service that could be provided (maybe a dream analyzer!). We'll be acting out these commercials for the class, or if you prefer, you can sign out one of the AV Club cameras and film your ad to show in class.

As part of the assignment, provide the written direction of your commercial.

Due: April 23

▶▶ ▶▶ ▶▶

From: Von Ipo (thenexteastwood@hotmail.com)
To: Arthur Bean (arthuraaronbean@gmail.com)
Sent: April 4, 15:06

Hey, Arthur!

I was talking to some of the other Leg Breakers, and we thought maybe we could hang out this weekend. Maybe tomorrow? We can do it here at my house. My basement is basically the same size as the Drama room it's so big, so we can push the couches aside and rehearse a few of the plays if we want to, or we can just hang out. My parents don't mind. After, we could watch a movie too. We've got a huge TV. It's basically the same as going to the movies!

Let me know. I can get the gang together!

Cheers!
Von

From: Arthur Bean (arthuraaronbean@gmail.com)
To: Von Ipo (thenexteastwood@hotmail.com)
Sent: April 4, 18:22

Dear Von,

I could probably make that work. I'm pretty busy, but I might be able to fit that in as well.

Arthur Bean

From: Von Ipo (thenexteastwood@hotmail.com)
To: Arthur Bean (arthuraaronbean@gmail.com)
Sent: April 4, 18:45

Hey, Arthur!

Great! Everyone else said they could come already. This is going to be awesome! I think we should rehearse, don't you? I bet Kraleigh thinks that she can say she'll reinstate our plays later and that we won't do them because we won't be ready to perform. Did you know that she's pulled me into her office three times because I was late for school? I told her once that it was the fault of the bed company for making it too cozy, but she didn't think that was funny at all. After that, I told her that I'm up late studying because I have to work really hard to be good at stuff. It's a total lie, but at least it got me out of trouble. Ha!

See you tomorrow!
Von

▶▶ ▶▶ ▶▶

April 7th

Dear RJ,

This weekend was pretty epic. A bunch of the Leg Breakers hung at Von's house, and it was great, other than Von being there. His house is really big. Bigger than Kennedy's, even. He's got a ton of stuff too, but of course, he had to show off all of it. It was really annoying, because he has to tell you how much everything costs and how important it is, blah, blah, blah. It took us forever to get started with rehearsing too, because he was showing off all this stuff he has.

Then on Sunday, I practised fencing with Millie and Joie. Millie said that she would help me with my *Macbeth* commercial too, and we could put in a fencing scene, and do the big battle between Macbeth and Macduff at the end. Since Macduff kills Macbeth, I wrote in a joke about it too. Joie's going to film it for us. We're going to make it so realistic since we'll have a real fencing match. It's going to be a commercial for Kevlar, which is bulletproof and swordproof material. It's going to be really funny. Robbie will be here to help too, so it's going to be epic!

I finally felt like I had a bunch of friends this weekend. I think this must be how Kennedy feels all the time, being so popular and having a bunch of friends to hang out with.

Yours truly,
Arthur Bean

April 10th

Dear RJ,

We had a Leg Breakers meeting today, and we told Hark that we would definitely not do Kraleigh's puberty musical. I did most of the talking again. I really think the other Leg Breakers see me as kind of their leader, which is amazing. I told him that we respected him as a teacher, but that we felt strongly that our plays should be put on, and that we were going to perform our plays, despite what Kraleigh wanted.

There were a few arguments in the group, and some of the students really didn't want to do their plays since they were banned. Now we aren't going to do their plays, and we'll only put on the ones that people want to do. We made sure that everyone got a chance to decide, and so far we're going to do six of the plays, and three people are still deciding.

Some of the kids said that they didn't want to do the plays because they didn't want to get in trouble. I tried to explain to them that if we were all involved, then there was less chance that they would get in trouble, and that we should stick together and be strong defenders of freedom of speech.

Hark said that he understood how we felt, but that he wouldn't be involved in any programming, and said that we were embarking on our own.

After the meeting, a bunch of us stayed and

talked about how we should get more support by showing the other students scenes from our plays when they aren't expecting it. Maybe if they see how tame the scenes are, they will join our cause.

It's so exciting! I've never been such a rebel before!

Yours truly,
Arthur Bean

▶▶ ▶▶ ▶▶

Hey, Artie,

Come by my class after school today so that we can chat about your next article for the Marathon. I heard through the staff grapevine that you may be planning something rather controversial. I'd like us to cover our bases BEFORE you start writing.

Cheers!
Mr. E.

Dear Mr. Everett,

I'm really sorry. I won't be able to make it!

Yours truly,
Arthur Bean

▶▶ ▶▶ ▶▶

JOGO: The Show Must Go On!

By Arthur Bean

There was recently some drama in the Drama room that you may have heard about. The administration of our fine school decided that the plays written and directed by the grade nine Leg Breakers playwriting group were inappropriate for public viewing. Some of the Leg Breakers strongly disagree with the administration, so we have decided to continue with the play festival.

We know that the administration thinks differently than we do, but we don't want to be quiet. Some of our plays may be rated M for Mature if they were movies, but they aren't movies. They're plays. It says right in the name that they are meant for entertainment. We're just playing.

You'll get a chance to decide for yourself if you want to join the Leg Breakers and our defence of free speech. Who knows? Maybe you'll be eating lunch one day and happen upon a scene or two of us rehearsing out on the field. Or maybe we'll be a dramatic flash mob during your Gym class. Anything can happen!

My mom always said, "playing is some of the best learning," so please consider joining us, the Leg Breakers Rebel Forces. Grade sevens and grade eights will also be considered as new recruits. If you aren't ready to be part of the solution, show your support in June by coming to our play festival. Plus, I bet you'll laugh. Our plays are really great. But hey, that's . . .

Just One Guy's Opinion.

Mr. Bean,

See me in my office immediately.

R. Kraleigh

▶▶ ▶▶ ▶▶

I got told that I have to print a retraction and apology in the newspaper for one of my articles.

i dont know what that means

Kraleigh pulled me into her office and said that I had to publicly retract my call to action about getting more members to join the Leg Breakers, or else!!

or else what? u get suspended??

She said that "the actions of a few can cause implications for many." I don't know what she means, but it sounds kind of vague.

yeah. empty threat. i say dont do it

Don't do the plays?

no, dont do the retraction thing

I totally agree!

April 17th

Dear RJ,

I told the gang about what Kraleigh told me yesterday, and they were so mad. It was great, because I was kind of scared by what she said, but Ben thinks that she's bluffing. He said that she's just trying to scare us (and it totally worked on me!) and that we should call her bluff. Millie agreed with him, and so did Latha. A few of the other Leg Breakers said that they didn't want to do their plays anymore, so we're down to five plays, and the three who weren't sure are definitely going to be out now.

Ben said that we should put up our scenes right after Easter in the cafeteria at lunch. When he suggested that, we all agreed. It makes me feel queasy, though. I'm really nervous. It's one thing to write an article about it. This will be going directly against Kraleigh's orders. I'm hoping that maybe it's just because I'm excited about the idea, not scared! No one else seemed scared about the idea, except the kids who dropped out. And I definitely don't want to drop out of the group. They need me!

Yours truly,
Arthur Bean

Happy Easter!

u 2 man

Thanks for your help with my commercial. It looks amazing.

i do look good in a wig

Your witch is the funniest by far.

i try

Are you and your dad doing anything for dinner tonight? My dad and I are going for Chinese food. Want to come?

can caleb come 2?

Probably. I'll ask.

Yes. We're going at 6. Dad says we can pick you guys up!

cool

▶▶ ▶▶ ▶▶

Assignment: *Macbeth* Commercial

By Arthur Bean

(Scene: Battlefield. *We zoom in on Macbeth and Macduff. They are fencing in an epic fight. Macbeth gets stabbed by Macduff.*)

Voiceover: Hath this ever happened to thou? *(Zoom in on Macbeth. He nods as he is dying.)*

Voiceover: Then thou needeth a new brocade! Check out these newest fabrics, made of Kevlar, the strongest of all fabrics.

Macbeth: I do need that! But where do I get it?

Voiceover: Kevlar is made from the brew of three of the best witches East Calgary has ever seen.

(The commercial cuts to three witches around a cauldron. They are stirring a giant pot.)

Witch One: Double Double . . . knit and purl.

Witch Two: Made from wool of bat and tongue of dog. Very strong stuff!

Witch Three: And designed with the latest fashion in mind!

Witch One: Fit for a king!

Witch Two: Or a king *murderer*!

Witch Three: Did I mention how fashionable it is? I designed it myself. (*Other witches groan.*)

Witch One, Two and Three (*pull the Kevlar vest out of the pot*): Abracadabra!

(They all look at each other.)

Witch Three: Looks like we're done here. (*Pause.*) When shall we three meet again?

(The commercial cuts back to Macbeth and Macduff. Macbeth is almost dead.)

Macbeth: Why didn't they give me that when I last visited them?

Voiceover: Because thou didn't ask for it by name.

Macbeth: I thought I couldn't be killed.

Macduff: Silly Macbeth. The prophecy TOLD you I could kill you. Too bad you didn't understand earlier and get some Kevlar.

(*Macbeth dies. Macduff turns to the camera.*)

Macduff (*shows off the Kevlar under his coat*): Kevlar. Unlike Macbeth, it's a name you can trust.

The End

Arthur,

Your video made me laugh out loud today. I appreciate how much work you put into your script and the filming of your commercial. It was nice to see Robbie Zack making a cameo appearance as one of the witches. He's such a tall young man now!
    Well done!

Ms Whitehead

▶▶ ▶▶ ▶▶

April 24th

Dear RJ,

We did a couple of scenes from our plays today, and it was crazy! We were in the cafeteria, and it was kind of like a flash mob. First, Latha started talking really loudly, saying lines from one of the plays, then Ben joined in and stood up, and then a few more people joined, and then the rest of us joined in. We really only had time to do a couple of parts from Ben's play, and I'm not in that one, so I was just in the group that stood behind them in solidarity. Then we all yelled, "The Leg Breakers!!" and then Ben did a little speech about coming to our rebel play festival and supporting free speech. A bunch of people clapped, and then we went back to our seats.

Ben did most of the talking, because I didn't want to always be the one at the very front. I told him that he had the loudest voice, and he's so tall that maybe Kraleigh would be scared of him, but actually, I just didn't want to be the one to do it. I was worried that I would get suspended from school on the spot or something. It's kind of like in *Macbeth*. He gets spurred on to kill the king by his wife, but then he regrets it after and has nightmares and dies. I'd rather be Lady Macbeth. (Not actually a lady, though. Come on!) She just tells him what to do, but never has to do the dirty work. I like that idea better. I don't really want to be the face of a revolution.

The thing was, Kraleigh wasn't there. Avril the lunch lady and Mr. Everett were the only adults there. So I don't know if it was even worth it.

Yours truly,
Arthur Bean

▶▶ ▶▶ ▶▶

April 25th

Dear RJ,

Well, clearly Kraleigh found out about our guerrilla theatre yesterday. She called an assembly for all the grade nines today. She said that a small group of grade nines "felt compelled to ruin the image of the school" and that she was cancelling our grad celebrations because of it. RJ, I'd never actually heard what an "uproar" sounds like, but I heard one today. Kraleigh couldn't get control of the group again for fifteen minutes, because people were yelling, and some girls (including Kennedy) ran out of the room, crying. She said that we still had the power to turn things around, and that we should think "long and hard" about the choices that we make.

I can't believe she actually cancelled grad! There's still a bunch of us who were going to do our plays, but now I don't know what's going to happen. I kind of wish that we had never written plays to begin with.

I wonder how much Kennedy thinks this was my fault. It's not all my fault. I hope she's not mad at me.

Yours truly,
Arthur Bean

From: Kennedy Laurel (imsocutekl@hotmail.com)
To: Arthur Bean (arthuraaronbean@gmail.com)
Sent: April 25, 17:20

I SWEAR, you are TRYING to ruin my life, Arthur Bean!!! You know, I totally get that you felt wronged and stuff, but you CANNOT go around doing whatever you want and ruining other people's lives for your own stupid cause! You know I already have my grad dress?!?! What am I supposed to do with that?!?

You know how HARD the grad committee and I have been working!! It's in the newspaper! I talk about it ALL THE TIME!!

I've been working this year on being a LEADER. Being a LEADER means CHOOSING BEST FOR THE TEAM. Maybe you should try it???

I supported you when you said that it was all about free speech, but now I think you're just trying to show off with your dumb friends and your dumb plays! I don't know what is going on in your head sometimes! I thought you were really smart, but it turns out, you're MEAN and THOUGHTLESS!

Kennedy

From: Arthur Bean (arthuraaronbean@gmail.com)
To: Kennedy Laurel (imsocutekl@hotmail.com)
Sent: April 25, 17:36

Dear Kennedy,

I'm sorry!!! It's not about you! It's all a misunderstanding! All we want is to do our plays. If you could see them, you would understand. Haven't you ever been really proud of something and then had it pulled away from you and told that you shouldn't be proud of it?

   Don't worry. I'm sure grad will happen. By Monday, Kraleigh will have calmed down, and grad will be back on. She'll come around. She has to; we're totally right about this whole thing. She just needs time to see it!

Yours truly,
Arthur Bean

▶▶ ▶▶ ▶▶

i got the job!

What job?

as a jr counciler at flying spirit camp

What?! How have they made all their decisions already? You're going back to camp this year?

ya but this time i get paid!

Do you know if they're still hiring? I could be a counsellor too, maybe.

dude i applied in winter. i doubt that they are still hiring

So, that's it? You're going to work at camp all summer? What am I going to do?

be a camper who has to do all my chores haha

This is a disaster! I can't believe they are done hiring for counsellors! I wonder if they would hire me because they know me. I'd be an awesome counsellor!

u could ask

I'm going to!

▶▶ ▶▶ ▶▶

From: Von Ipo (thenexteastwood@hotmail.com)
To: Arthur Bean (arthuraaronbean@gmail.com)
Sent: April 27, 9:58

Hey, Arthur!

Crazy day on Friday, hey? I still say we stick to our guns! My auntie works for the CBC news, and she said that we could meet with her if we wanted to do something for the news. It would basically be the headline news if we want. Can you imagine? Kraleigh would lose it! I bet she doesn't think we would do it!

Anyway, the gang's all coming over this aft to rehearse and we can plan what our next move is. You free? We could basically film a whole news piece if we want. We can use one of my video cameras!

Let me know! Cheers!

Von

April 27th

Dear RJ,

I spent all weekend worrying about the Leg Breakers and the grad being cancelled. I told Kennedy that Kraleigh would change her mind over the weekend, but what if she doesn't? Did I get the whole grad cancelled? I mean, I'm the one who wrote the articles about being censored. And what if everyone else starts to hate me the way Kennedy does? The whole school could turn against me. What if all the Leg Breakers have changed their minds over the weekend, and it's just me and Von? I'll have no friends again. And I really like the Leg Breakers gang. I want to hang out with them still!

Yours truly,
Arthur Bean

▸▸ ▸▸ ▸▸

From: Arthur Bean (arthuraaronbean@gmail.com)
To: Kennedy Laurel (imsocutekl@hotmail.com)
Sent: April 29, 19:06

Dear Kennedy,

OK, so Kraleigh didn't change her mind yet, but did you see the Leg Breakers Stand Up! posters that were up today? I didn't have anything to do with those, but clearly there are other students who think that we are right!

Yours truly,
Arthur Bean

▸▸ ▸▸ ▸▸

Assignment: *Macbeth* Review

We'll be attending the matinee of Theatre Calgary's *Macbeth* on Friday. This is an excellent opportunity to see Shakespeare come alive onstage! I want you to keep notes about what you like and don't like about the production. Things to keep in mind:

How are the characters the same or different from how you pictured them?

How well does the set work?

What themes are they trying to emphasize in the production? How do you know this?

How do the costumes and lights add to or distract from the play?

How easy is it to know what is happening?

Who is your favourite character in the production? Is he/she different than your favourite character when we read the play?

Due: May 8

MAY

From: Kennedy Laurel (imsocutekl@hotmail.com)
To: Arthur Bean (arthuraaronbean@gmail.com)
Sent: May 1, 18:23

Arthur!

You have to stop your fight against Ms Kraleigh!!!
She's NEVER going to back down! It's NOT FAIR!!
I've worked SO HARD on grad and now you and your
friends come in and ruin it?! I don't know what your
problem is! They are just little plays! You've written
THOUSANDS of things, so why do you care about
this one so much?!?

Kennedy

From: Arthur Bean (arthuraaronbean@gmail.com)
To: Kennedy Laurel (imsocutekl@hotmail.com)
Sent: May 1, 20:50

Dear Kennedy,

I wish you could see the bigger picture here! It's
not just me. Maybe you don't understand the whole
story; it's not just about our plays, it's a question
of free speech! I know you care about this too,

otherwise you wouldn't be on the newspaper. You said that you supported us before. Don't give up now!

I wish I could help you, but this is too important. I'm basically the president of the Leg Breakers, and I need to stand by them.

Yours truly,
Arthur Bean

From: Kennedy Laurel (imsocutekl@hotmail.com)
To: Arthur Bean (arthuraaronbean@gmail.com)
Sent: May 1, 21:32

But Arthur, it's NOT about your plays anymore! It's about the fact that you were told not to do something, and you did it anyway!! *That's* the problem!! I BET that you would have been allowed to do the plays if you guys hadn't been SO STUPID about doing them in the cafeteria and writing that dumb article!

Kennedy

▶▶ ▶▶ ▶▶

May 4th

Dear RJ,

Two more people joined our Leg Breakers Stand Up! group today. (That's what we're calling ourselves. I thought of it. I think it's pretty

184

funny.) Akaya and Yolande said that they wanted to be part of it, so Von invited them to our rehearsal. I don't exactly know how we're going to get them to be part of it, but I guess we can write more parts into the plays for them. We rehearsed for most of the afternoon, and then after that, Millie and I met Joie and we worked on my Social Studies presentation. I got special permission to have Millie help me do my presentation on the Plains of Abraham even though she's in the other class. We're going to re-enact the fight scenes between the French and the English. That way, we can fence in class! It's going to be awesome. I'm actually getting to be pretty good at fencing. Deeter said that I have a good chance of doing well at the competition in June. That would be awesome. It's cool, because I think I look pretty badass with all the bruises on my arms and legs. Robbie said that it just looks like I lose a lot because I'm clearly getting stabbed, but I told him that everyone gets hit on the arms and legs, and it's the shots to the kill zone (chest and back) that count in foil fencing. (It's not actually called the kill zone, but I like to say that because it annoys Deeter so much!)

Yours truly,
Arthur Bean

▶▶ ▶▶ ▶▶

May 5th

Dear RJ,

Just giving you a history lesson here. It turns out the Plains of Abraham battle wasn't fought as much with swords as with cannons. I definitely don't have a cannon. Maybe we can do something with spitballs?

Also, I think Kennedy really hates me. I tried to talk to her, and she won't even acknowledge that I exist. I hate that she hates me. I don't like knowing that there are people who hate me. I want everyone to like me. But mostly, I really want Kennedy to like me.

Yours truly,
Arthur Bean

▶▶ ▶▶ ▶▶

Hey, Artie,

I'd love it if we could meet today and discuss what you were thinking about posting in your JOGO article this week.

Cheers!
Mr. E.

▶▶ ▶▶ ▶▶

JOGO: Standing Together

By Arthur Bean

There are times when we have to choose sides. I think that being in junior high is practice for being adults. From what I know about voting, there's never a perfect option, but it's important to choose anyway. (At least, that's what my friend Anila would say. My dad says that when you vote, you vote for the least terrible person out of a sea of terrible people.)

There will be more times in our lives when we have to choose between two options that aren't perfect. The way I see it, the best option is to choose what your friends are choosing. This way there won't be as many arguments, and you'll still have friends.

The more people that believe in the same thing you do, the easier it is to believe in it yourself. Sure, maybe you'll go home and wonder if you've made the right choice, but the next day you'll be back with your friends and realize that it's not so hard if you all stick together.

So, when you choose, choose your friends. But hey, that's . . .

Just One Guy's Opinion.

Hey, Artie,

This article is an interesting choice of subject. It's vague though; I'm not sure if our readers will fully understand what you're trying to convey — that you make a choice on principle and stick to it, or you side with the majority. I think we can work on making your point clearer and more focused!

Mr. E.

Assignment: *Macbeth* **Review**

By Arthur Bean

Theatre Calgary's version of *Macbeth* was a hot mess that left me cold.

First of all, I hated that they modernized it. Making it all about Canadian politics was a terrible choice. I wanted to see epic sword-fighting scenes and giant, elaborate costumes. Instead, there were suits and cell phones. Adding technology was so stupid! I feel like they were trying to modernize the play so that kids would think it was cool, but instead, I think that adults are the most boring people on earth. Turning portions of the script into text messages on screens beside the stage meant watching the play was more like reading it. And take it from me, watching people text is about as interesting as watching paint dry.

And let's talk about the set. I hated the high platforms; I couldn't even see the witches. What a stupid choice to make; even amateur directors know that you shouldn't put the best parts of a play on parts of the stage that aren't visible from the crappy seats. Sure, we don't have a lot of money, but in Shakespeare's time, they made sure that the poor people could still see the play. Although, maybe the theatre company didn't have any money? That would explain the boring costumes and lame set that was designed to look like an office building. The only cool part of the whole thing was the glass elevator between the top level and the stage.

If they had no money, it would also explain why the acting was so bad. I was hoping there would be lots of screaming and crying, and there wasn't. Also, why was Lady Macbeth thirty years younger than Macbeth? It was just plain creepy.

I wish I could say more about the play, but I fell asleep in the second act, and only saw the last fight scene (which I would have done a way better job at, being a fencer and all). If this play had been interesting at all, I'm sure I would have stayed awake. I actually liked reading the play, and I was excited to see it. Now I'm annoyed that they wrecked the whole play for me. I'll never see it again.

Arthur,

I think you make some valid points here, but I feel you could have given a more thorough description of the production. What did you like about it? Who was your favourite character? How did modernizing the script bring out different aspects than you expected? You didn't speak to any of the themes of the play, or any of its strengths as a production. Focusing only on the look of the play and the staging of it isn't a complete picture of the production as a whole.

Ms Whitehead

▸▸ ▸▸ ▸▸

happy bday!!!!!

Thanks. It's been pretty lame. I had a Math test and Mr. Everett made me redo my Science questions.

that sounds like it sucked. r u having a party this weekend?

No. I wouldn't know who to invite anyway.

Awwww. someone is feeling sorry for himself . . .

No! I just don't care about my birthday.

(sad violins play)

You're a jerk. And you've always sucked at playing instruments.

(sad violins screech to a halt)

next year ill have a car and ill come visit

You won't be 16.

thats not gonna stop me!

Ha! Yeah right!

(packs up his violin and runs away)

▶▶ ▶▶ ▶▶

May 11th

Dear RJ,

I don't like where everything with the Leg Breakers
is going. Everyone at Von's house this afternoon
really wanted to stage a protest outside the school,
and invite the media to come and film it. They
are making a huge deal about the whole thing!
Things are going further than I wanted them to go.
I mean, I still think that we should be allowed to
do our plays, but I don't want to be on the news.
I think we could look like whiny teenagers. I've
seen how things get edited sometimes, and the
news is run by adults, so of course they are going
to make the adults look like they are the ones
who are right. I tried to explain this to everyone,
but then they asked if I was chickening out,
and Ben wanted to know if I was all talk and
no action. I really don't want to seem like I'm a
wimp, so I told them that we just needed to plan
out what to say and make sure that we don't say

anything that could be taken in the wrong way.

RJ, I don't know what to do. I want to stand up for what I believe in and free speech and all that, but I don't want Kennedy and half the class to hate me for being part of the group that got grad cancelled.

Yours truly,
Arthur Bean

r u around this weekend? im gonna come up

Really? I'm not going to be here!!

where r u going?!?! u have no life

That's what you think. My dad and I are going camping. Why are you coming up?

dad wants me 2. plus lethbridge is boring right now

Why is it so boring?

y r u so boring? thats just life

Do you want to come camping?

nope

It would be good practice for when you're a counsellor.

still nope, it might still be snowing in the mountains. u guys r crazy!

Well, I hope Calgary is really boring for you.

awwww ill miss u 2

▶▶ ▶▶ ▶▶

From: Kennedy Laurel (imsocutekl@hotmail.com)
To: Arthur Bean (arthuraaronbean@gmail.com)
Sent: May 18, 14:08

Arthur,

I was out this weekend and I heard that you guys are now planning a PROTEST for the news?!?! What gives?! You know that there are WAY more grade nines who care about grad than care about your plays, right?!? And if you put on your plays, NO ONE is going to come. I'll make sure of that!!

Can you PLEASE stop your group from ruining what SHOULD be the BEST DAY of junior high?!?!

Kennedy

▶▶ ▶▶ ▶▶

From: Kennedy Laurel (imsocutekl@hotmail.com)
To: Arthur Bean (arthuraaronbean@gmail.com)
Sent: May 19, 10:50

I can't believe you won't even respond to me now. SERIOUSLY? That's so immature!

Kennedy

From: Arthur Bean (arthuraaronbean@gmail.com)
To: Kennedy Laurel (imsocutekl@hotmail.com)
Sent: May 19, 21:37

Dear Kennedy,

I swear, I'm not avoiding you! I was away all weekend, and I just got home and saw your emails. And we're not doing a protest. You shouldn't believe everything you hear. It's totally overblown.

I wish you understood how important it is to some of the Leg Breakers that we do the plays. It's a big deal. It's about our rights!! You know that I would never do anything to hurt you, and if it was up to me, I would do something about it. But there's nothing I can do now. It's too big!

If you want, maybe you and I could get together after school one day and figure out the best thing to make it all work out for everyone. I bet if we brainstormed, we could come up with some really great ideas. You and I work so well together!

Yours truly,
Arthur Bean

May 19th

Dear RJ,

I wish I had fencing tonight. I could really have used the distraction. Instead, I'm just sitting at home, freaking out about the Leg Breakers. Von has been suspiciously silent all weekend, which makes me think he's doing something weird and awful, like building a giant platform for some national news story. I wish we hadn't gone away this weekend. It feels like we were gone for a month, not just three days. Plus, Dad takes our phones and locks them in the glove box of the car so that we can "power down" while we're camping. But now look where it's got me. Kennedy is furious, and I have no idea what the Leg Breakers did this weekend! Next time we go, I'm going to insist I keep my phone with me. It's necessary for my survival!!

Yours truly,
Arthur Bean

▶▶ ▶▶ ▶▶

Assignment: Book Review Three

An Antarctic Odyssey
by Nick Bertozzi

This is my third and final book review for you, Ms Whitehead. I hope that you are moved to tears by my most touching and sincere book review here.

My last choice is to review *An Antarctic Odyssey* by Nick Bertozzi.

I got this book for my birthday from my best friend in Lethbridge. He's really into comics and normally I don't like the same stuff he does. But he said that he had never read this book, and he was told by the bookstore owner that it wasn't like a comic.

First off, I should assure you that this fits into the non-fiction that you wanted us to read. Frankly, I never read non-fiction, because normally I read the first chapter, or paragraph, or heck, even just the title and subtitle, and I figure that I know what the book is about. I don't understand how people need 300 pages to describe how to make cheese or the history of salt. I get it. Salt was important.

This book made me think, "Why aren't all non-fiction books illustrated like graphic novels?" It's so much easier to read them. I finished this one in an hour, tops. If I were in charge of Social Studies textbooks, I would make them all comic strips featuring a talking guinea pig named Scott. Scott could narrate all the cool stuff that happened in history, rather than long boring passages about the Fall of France. And I would show Scott getting killed in ways that match how different people died during the different battles. At the end of every chapter, Scott the Time-Travelling Guinea Pig would be stabbed, or beheaded, or shot through with an arrow, or something equally historic.

Anyway, the book was all right. I still don't like non-fiction books, but I liked the parts when they almost got eaten by the giant sea monster, and watched whales breed. I found all the characters confusing. They all looked the same.

I give this book a 70%.

Arthur,

Your book review doesn't say much about the book. In fact, you say almost nothing about the book, the synthesis of information, the language level, your engagement with the narrative or any of the criteria of the assignment. I get the feeling that you didn't actually read this book, which is not like you at all. For one thing, Shackleton and his crew were never beset by a sea monster. Perhaps, the next time you read a graphic work of any kind, spend more than an hour focusing on the illustrations and the interplay between word and picture. There's a lot more to be gleaned from books like this than what's written in the text!

Ms Whitehead

▶▶ ▶▶ ▶▶

May 22nd

Dear RJ,

We're two weeks away from when we were going to put our plays on. Do you think it's too late to drop out? Von said that he's going to have a news crew at the school Monday morning to cover the story, and he wants me to do the talking, because according to him, I started the whole thing. I would like to state for the record, I didn't start it! The way I see it, Kraleigh started it. But it doesn't matter now, because I sure don't want to be on camera! Kennedy has put up posters all around the school, on top of our Leg Breakers posters, and they all say *Graduation Celebration, Not Theatrical Vexation!* The posters tell people that they should boycott our play night.

RJ, I never thought that writing one article and stating my opinion would go this far. And now so many other people are getting upset, all because of me. I don't know whether I made a huge mistake, or if it's worth it, because you *should* stand up for yourself. I do know that I don't want to do this anymore. I want all of it to be over, and I don't want Kennedy to hate me, and I don't want to worry that Hark is going to quit because of me, and I definitely, DEFINITELY don't want to hang out at Von's house anymore.

Yours truly,
Arthur Bean

▶▶ ▶▶ ▶▶

Assignment: Extreme Survival!

Oh no! Your character is in a life or death situation! It's up to you and your newfound technical writing skills to guide your character to safety. It doesn't matter how ridiculous the situation you choose may be; what you'll be graded on is your clear explanations, organization and logic.

Remember the tips for good practical writing:

1. Be clear
2. Be detailed
3. Be logical
4. Use simple sentences
5. Use the present tense

Due: June 6

▶▶   ▶▶   ▶▶

did u get a job at camp?

Not yet. I should probably get on that.

i got my contract in the mail today so its probly too late

u know that camp starts in a month right?

No. It's not until the second week of July.

not if u work there, we start june 30

I'm sure it's fine.

riiiiight

JUNE

June 1st

Dear RJ,

Barely anyone showed up to the Leg Breakers rehearsal today. Even Ben and Latha didn't come, and they've come to all of them. Everyone seemed really . . . I actually don't know how to describe it. It was like everyone was defeated or tired or something. Well, everyone except Von. Von said that we needed to keep our energy up even though it's exam season. He said that people couldn't come because they were studying, but I know that no one actually studies for exams for a whole month before them. You maybe, MAYBE, read over the textbook a couple of times the week before, but I don't think Ben would even do that. He's one of those naturally perfect guys who is smart and funny and all the girls love him no matter what. I'm surprised that he and Kennedy haven't gone out. They'd probably be the perfect couple. Don't tell them that, though. Or maybe they wanted to date, but it was too awkward because Kennedy and I went out, and Ben's a friend of mine and said that he couldn't do that to me. See, RJ? That's the kind of thing that Ben would do. He's just that kind of guy.

But more to the point, I wonder if everyone else is thinking the same thing that I am.

What if no one wants to do it anymore? I can't ask them, because I don't want to be the quitter, but what if everyone is writing the same things in their journals at home? The only one who seems really keen still is Von, which is totally unsurprising, since he's so lame and doesn't get it.

Yours truly,
Arthur Bean

▶▶ ▶▶ ▶▶

From: Kennedy Laurel (imsocutekl@hotmail.com)
To: Arthur Bean (arthuraaronbean@gmail.com)
Sent: June 2, 19:14

Arthur,

I wanted to let you know that I'm going to write a feature article for the Grad Matters! campaign that Catie and I started. I already asked Mr. E. if we could put it on the front page, ESPECIALLY since you got two of your articles featured that got us in this whole mess. Of course, he said yes.

I'm going to prove to Ms Kraleigh that I'm a true leader around here. I've already told her that you and I are NOT friends or on the same side, just to make sure I can win that award. If I don't, you can consider this friendship 100% OVER.

Kennedy

From: Arthur Bean (arthuraaronbean@gmail.com)
To: Kennedy Laurel (imsocutekl@hotmail.com)
Sent: June 2, 20:58

Dear Kennedy,

I agree. You should put your article on the front page.
The *Marathon* is fully committed to showing both
sides to every story! I'm not writing anything this
week, so you don't have to worry about me!

Yours truly,
Arthur Bean

▶▶   ▶▶   ▶▶

June 3rd

Dear RJ,

I emailed Tomasz at camp and asked him
about the camp counsellor job for the summer,
but I got an email back today saying that they
filled all the positions. How could that be? I
was SURE that he would make room for me;
I was one of the best campers! I was one of
the best dish washers (nobody else washed
the underside of the plates or bowls), I always
participated at campfire, and I even helped out
the seven-year-olds when they needed someone
to tie their shoes or do up their life jackets. I'd
be a great counsellor! Now Robbie's going to be
at camp all summer, and I'm going to be left

doing nothing! This summer is going to suck and it hasn't even started. I think it's going to be a worse summer than the one after Mom died, and that one was horrible!

What if Dad makes me get a job in the city? That would be the worst. I guess I should look for jobs myself. I wonder what kinds of jobs I could get as a writer. Maybe in an ad agency? I could write pretty good slogans.

Yours truly,
Arthur Bean
Arthur Bean: It's Bean a Pleasure
Arthur Bean: The Importance of Bean, Arthur
Arthur Bean: Top of the Stalk

▶▶ ▶▶ ▶▶

> Are you going to be here for my fencing competition?

> probly not when is it?

> June 15. It's all day.

> no way my mom woud let me come its exams time

> plus its hayleys moms bday and were making the cake

> You're still dating Hayley?

of course dumass when woud we have brokn up???

I don't know.

im a gentleman. i treat a girl right

in fact, u could take some lessons from me

Sure. What else would you teach me?

art. football. mad life skills

Not spelling, I hope.

no need artie. thats what spelchek is 4

June 5th

Dear RJ,

I gave in, RJ. I had to. Time is running out, and I know how much Kennedy wants the grad to happen, and even Millie was talking about how sad it would be if we didn't have a Grad Dance! So I skipped Gym (because any reason to miss long-distance running is a good reason), and had a meeting with Kraleigh. I told her that I wanted to put on our plays, but I wanted grad to happen too, and that I felt that we could come to a compromise. And you know what, RJ? She COMPLIMENTED me. She said that she felt I was showing some real maturity in coming to speak to her. It was so condescending that I almost left right then and there. But then she kept talking. She asked me what I felt would be a reasonable compromise. I was trapped. I figured that she was the adult, and that she would be the one to come up with the idea, not me! I didn't have any ideas, so she said that I should talk to my friends and come up with what we felt would be a reasonable compromise for the plays, and she would seriously consider our request.

Then she said something totally shocking. She said that I reminded her a lot of my mom. I had no idea she knew my mom! Kraleigh said that they used to work together a long time ago, and she always respected how my mom stood up for what she believed in. She told me that my mom got the admin to agree to some kind of big change in their report card schedule (I didn't really understand what she meant) in the school they worked in. Then Kraleigh actually said, "I bet you miss her. It's right around June that she died, isn't it?"

RJ, no one ever acknowledges her death head-on like that. People always skate around the fact that she died, and no one ever says to my face, "Your mom is dead." It's like they are scared that I'll start bawling in their face. Yeah, because that's going to happen!

But Kraleigh was so straightforward about it that I said, "Yeah. She died three years ago on Saturday. Not that it matters. I feel the same about it every day anyway."

She nodded, and told me her mom died a few years ago as well, which I didn't think was as big a deal, because Kraleigh is way older than me. But the more I think about it, the more I realize that it doesn't really matter how old you are when your mom dies. She's still your mom, and she's still dead, so it still sucks.

Yours truly,
Arthur Bean

▶▶ ▶▶ ▶▶

Assignment: Extreme Survival!

By Arthur Bean

Oh no! Odie Oderdonk is about to die!

How is he going to die, you ask? I'm glad you did.

Odie Oderdonk is a miner by trade, just like his father, Brodie Oderdonk, was before him, and his grandfather, Cody Oderdonk, before him.

And now Odie Oderdonk has tunnelled too deep and he is trapped. He can't get out!

Luckily, I can save you, Odie.

The first thing you need to do is breathe normally. If you start to hyperventilate, you'll use up all your oxygen and you'll die.

Next, look for the canary. There should be a canary in the mine with you. It will likely be in the upper left-hand quadrant of your hole if you are facing the wall. Pet the canary nicely to see if it's alive. If it is still alive, you have a chance of living. If it's not on its perch in the upper left-hand quadrant, then it is likely on the floor in the lower left-hand quadrant, and that is a bad sign, especially for the canary.

Odie, you say it's on its perch! Great news! Now take the canary and put it on your right shoulder. It needs saving as much as you do, and when you get out of here, you'll need someone who was in the trenches with you to commiserate.

Your next step is going to be trickier. You need to assess your surroundings. When you're assessing them, these are the four things you should look for:

1. Any hissing gases coming from anywhere (anywhere)
2. Any dead miners (below you)

3. A ladder (above you)
4. The pickaxe you dropped before you got stuck (below you, I hope)

Pick up the pickaxe. You may need it. Attach it to your jaunty snakeskin belt that you got for Christmas.

Now, take the dead miners, and stack them on top of each other until you have reached the bottom of the ladder. This next part may make you a bit queasy, but you need to step on the other people to get to the ladder. Once you reach the bottom rung, grab it with your hands. Now climb the ladder.

As you climb, you may notice that it's getting lighter above you. That's a good sign. If it's getting darker, then you are going down the ladder, and you must reverse direction.

The ladder may not go all the way to the top of the hole. That's OK; just keep breathing normally. Pull out your pickaxe from your jaunty snakeskin belt. Dig the pickaxe into the crusty dirt wall in front of you (where the ladder would be). Pull yourself up, until you see the smiling face of your wife, Dodie Oderdonk, peering down at you. When you see her, put one arm up and scream as loud as you can, "GET ME OUT OF HERE!!!"

Arthur,

I knew I could count on you to make this exercise in practical writing an exercise in pointing out the ridiculous.

If you take out the narrative that you've created for Odie Oderdonk, you've done a nice job on the practical writing here. However, I would like to see more focus on the task at hand, and less on building Odie's backstory. I know you can spin a good yarn; now show me how you can scale that back and hone specific writing skills needed for the real world.

Ms Whitehead

Dear Ms Whitehead,

I know what you're saying, but I think that telling stories is an important skill for the real world. I'm planning to leave the boring writing to other people. I bet Agatha Christie never had to write computer manuals.

Yours truly,
Arthur Bean

June 6th

Dear RJ,

I looked through all the Leg Breakers scripts
that we were going to perform. (Not that there's
that many left. With so many people dropping
out, we were down to three plays anyway.) I
think I've figured out what we can do. If we
make the guns into swords in my play, then
there won't be any gun violence, and we can
still do it. Plus, Millie and I can teach everyone
a few fencing moves, and we can make it look
really good, I think. In fact, I'm not sure why
I didn't think of it before! It will be way more
theatrical this way. I'll have to play one of the
parts, but that's OK. I already know all the
lines. Then if we do Ben and Latha's play, we
just have to take out the swear words, and
pretend like it's an R-rated movie that's on TV.
Hopefully the others agree. Please don't have
them kick me out!!

 I just hope that Kennedy realizes what we're
giving up for her. I'm sacrificing my principles to
the principal!

Yours truly,
Arthur Bean

▸▸ ▸▸ ▸▸

hey man i dont know what im supposed to say to u today

I don't know, either. May the Force be with you?

im not saying that, altho maybe that works? i dont know

r u guys doing anything?

Dad's at yoga, and I'm going to hang out with Millie and Joie later. I think we're going to a movie.

We got invited to this afternoon tea one of my mom's friends is having, but Dad and I agreed that that sounded like the worst thing ever.

puke a billion times over

Right?!?

well, good luck getting through the day. i hope the movie is funny

Me too, man. Me. Too.

▶▶ ▶▶ ▶▶

June 8th

Dear RJ,

Two things. First: The Leg Breakers met today, and we made some changes to our plays, so hopefully Kraleigh says OK and lets us go ahead with them. I'm going to talk to her tomorrow, and Ben and Von are going to come with me this time. Von's the only one who seemed annoyed by the fact that I talked to her without telling anyone. He thinks we are selling out, but I don't think he even knows what it means to sell out. Plus, everyone seemed kind of relieved. Maybe I'm just assuming they are relieved because I am, but I don't care.

Second: Yesterday at dinner, my dad started talking about the summer and how this is my last summer where he doesn't expect me to work. He kept talking about getting a summer job, and starting to make my own money, and I told him that I was trying to get a job at Flying Spirit as a camp counsellor. But he told me not to bother. Then he pulled out two plane tickets to Whitehorse. So I guess we're going to the Yukon to go camping for a month! I asked if we could rent a dogsled to get around, but apparently you can only do that in the winter, so we're renting a truck. I don't even know what to expect. What is Yukon like in the summer? Are there going to be a lot of bears? How many books do I need to bring for a month of camping?

It's a pretty cool thing that he did that. I was even thinking today that even if Mom were around, she wouldn't have come. Camping is just this thing for me and my dad.

I half-wish Robbie or Luke could come with us, but still. It should be pretty cool. There'll be twenty-four hours of daylight there. Is it manly to buy an eye mask for sleeping? As of today, I'm going to sleep with the lights on in my room to get ready for the summer.

Although that's probably why I'm still awake and it's two in the morning.

Yours truly,
Arthur Bean

▶▶ ▶▶ ▶▶

June 9th

Dear RJ,

She said no! She said that we hadn't gone far enough with our changes. I showed her how many lines we changed, but she said that "two lines per play" was not a sufficient compromise. I thought we had it! I was sure that if we took out most of the swears, it would be fine. She said, "You're on the right track, but I need to see more." I bet she wants us to take out every joke too!

I really, really wanted to tell her what I really

thought about her refusal, but Ben kicked me under the desk as I started to talk, and then he said that we would revisit the work and come up with something else.

Instead, we're going to ask Hark to help us. I can't tell what's OK anymore anyway. I just hope he knows.

Yours truly,
Arthur Bean

▸▸ ▸▸ ▸▸

Hey, Artie,

What are you thinking of doing for your final article? It's a big one! This is your chance to pass on some of your hard-earned knowledge before heading off to high school. Kennedy's working on a double-page spread about the grad, and she's written a great little piece about hope and believing in yourself. So what do you think? Maybe an exposé about the music teacher getting the kids to read band books? (Please don't actually write that. That was a joke!)

Cheers!
Mr. E.

▸▸ ▸▸ ▸▸

June 13th

Dear RJ,

Kraleigh finally agreed to our modified plays. We changed the swords to lightsabers (so now we have to add in some lighting cues to make it dark onstage!), and for Von and Nigel's play, we took out the middle scene where the doctor eats the girl's intestines. That cut kind of sucks, since it's a big part of the play (it's called "Intestine Care Unit"), but their play isn't very good anyways. But now we can perform them at lunch the last week of school (which means that we can only do two a day, instead of a festival of all of them). But we get to perform them, which is good. Hark seemed really happy about it too, and said that we were being very mature. It still feels really weird, and I don't know if anyone will come, because people might still be mad about the grad stuff. But grad is back on, and Kennedy and her friends still get to decorate the gym and make their dumb slideshow of themselves or whatever else they are planning.

I'm a little mad about it, because Kennedy didn't say anything to me when she found out grad was back on. She could have thanked me or something. You know, I've tried all year to be nice to her and have her realize that I'm a good guy, and she never cares. I wish I didn't care so much about what she thought of me. Cool guys never care what people think of them.

Yours truly,
Arthur Bean

good luck! i bet youll be AWESOME

Thanks! I wish you could see me fence. Maybe you could take up fencing and then we could meet at competitions!

im more of a shrub guy

What? I don't get it.

instead of fences. i like shrubs, more inviting

But you know the old saying . . .

Good fencers make good neighbours!

u r a DORK

My joke is way better than your shrub joke.

I'm just telling it straight.

NOT BEATING AROUND THE BUSH

i was going to say that!! great minds

▶▶　▶▶　▶▶

June 14th

Dear RJ,

My fencing competition is tomorrow. I'm really nervous! I've been practising so much, and I even sometimes do footwork at the bus stop. (But not when other people are around, and really subtly. I don't want people to think I'm a total weirdo!) But still, I don't know what to expect. What if everyone is as good as Joie? What if my foil stops working in the middle of the bout, and so I get points, but they don't register on the lightbox? What if I get hit so hard that I have to go to the hospital?

Dad is going to come and watch, but I didn't invite anyone else. I almost told the Leg Breakers about it, because they wanted to meet to rehearse on Sunday, but then I don't want them to come, in case I lose. What was I thinking, signing up for a competition? I'm not an athlete. Maybe I won't go. I should probably not go.

Yours truly,
Arthur Bean

▶▶ ▶▶ ▶▶

> Guess what? I came in fourth at my fencing competition!

> thats awesome!!!!

I know! It was a pretty big deal as far as competitions go. All Calgary fencers were there!

olympics here u come

It was awesome. I won my first bout against this 15-year-old guy, and he didn't even score at all.

r u sure he was playing??

Yeah, I'm sure. He was hooked up and his sword was definitely working, because we tested it before we started. He was just really bad.

how many guys were fencing?

There were over 40 people at the whole competition.

ya but how many did u fence?

Do you mean how many guys, or people? Because the events are split male and female.

so how many in ur group?

Well, they are also split by age group, so I wasn't fencing all the adults.

so ur age group?

There were five of us.

so wait

u came in 2nd last?

HAHAHAHAHAHAHA

It sounds better if I say I came in fourth.

still laughing over here

It was my FIRST competition!

no worries dude. ur secret is safe with me. u came in forth

Personal Reflections: What Is Junior High?

You've almost made it! You've lived through three years of junior high and are soon off to the new challenges of high school.

Before you embark on the next step of your life adventure, take this assignment as an opportunity to reflect on the last three years. What middle-school experiences have affected you? How has your thinking changed over the last three years? What kind of advice would you pass on to a grade seven student starting junior high in September?

Due: June 25

From: Von Ipo (thenexteastwood@hotmail.com)
To: Arthur Bean (arthuraaronbean@gmail.com)
Sent: June 17, 17:24

Hey, Arthur!

So a bunch of the Leg Breakers are going to meet at my house before grad on Friday and go together. You're coming with us, right? Wouldn't be the same without you! We're basically going to show up like it's the red carpet. Ben said that we should all wear shades and walk in really slowly, like we're in a movie. Won't that be awesome?

Ben and Millie are going together, but they're still going to meet us here, so there'll be like eight of us. My mom can drive us, and Latha said that her dad might be able to drive the rest of us if we don't all fit in the car. I wanted to rent a limo, but my dad said no.

Which is so weird, because he basically lets me do whatever I want all the time.

Anyway, we're meeting at 5:00. Hope you can come!

Von

June 17th

Dear RJ,

Millie is going to grad with Ben? When did that happen? Are they together? She never said anything like that at fencing. I thought she liked Vincent. And what about Joie? Millie had said that she was taking Joie as her date to our grad. Does that mean that Joie's going alone? I know she's still coming; yesterday she was talking about the dress she was going to wear. I wonder if she's coming to Von's house as well. Maybe I should call and ask her if she wants a ride. Will she think that I like her? I've never hung out with just Joie. What if it's weird to not have Millie there? It's just a ride to a dumb dance. I should just call her, right, RJ? I'm being dumb. This is so stupid. We're just friends, and I'm just offering her a ride to Von's house because her place is on the way. I'm just being environmentally conscious. Right?

Yours truly,
Arthur Bean

June 17th

Dear RJ,

OK, I'm back. So I called Joie and asked her if she needed a ride to Von's house and she said yes. And then we talked for an hour on the phone, just about all kinds of other stuff. We talked about Millie and Ben, and they ARE together, and have been for two weeks, and they are already planning to go with Ben's parents to their family cabin for a week in July, so Joie said it sounds pretty serious. We talked about fencing, and we talked about how funny Bill Murray is (she's a huge fan) and she said that I should watch some Wes Anderson movies because they are really funny, and that they remind her of me. So now I have to know what these movies are like. She's really funny, RJ. I think she might be funnier than Millie. Together they are pretty hilarious, but she's actually funny by herself too.

Anyway, I'm going to pick her up to go to Von's together. Well, not together together, but just together.

Yours truly,
Arthur Bean

▸▸ ▸▸ ▸▸

JOGO: It's Time to Retire the Fox

By Arthur Bean

The band is playing, the crowd is pumped: the senior boys basketball final is about to start, and it looks like we're going to win this year — after all, we're playing Diefenbaker, and their star player has a groin injury. The energy is high, and then . . . in comes Terry.

Terry's looking worse for wear. The fox costume that has been recycled for over fifteen years is ready for retirement. It's been here longer than Mr. Kim, and I'm pretty sure he was teaching here before the Mounties created Fort Calgary. Terry the Fox is matted everywhere. His red coat of fur has turned puke brown-orange with age, and the papier mâché structure is showing under the armpits. He's been painted red to try and mask the damage done to Terry over the years, but I think it looks worse than seeing the bare spots. Not only that, but Terry the Fox stinks. Fifteen years of teenage boys running up and down the bleachers while inside the massive costume have taken their toll on all our olfactory senses. You can literally smell the fox before he even enters the gym. How is that supposed to inspire our athletes? The only thing I can think of is that they want to win quicker to get away from the steaming furry mess jumping on the sidelines of the big game.

So let's get rid of the pest, and while we're at it, why not update the mascot? Sure, it's easy to be the Terry Foxes, but couldn't we use a little imagination and be something more creative? I'm just thinking out loud here, but some of my suggestions are: the Gophers (they are consistently digging up our fields), the Leg Breakers (so dramatic, and so powerful!) or perhaps, and I'm just brainstorming here, the Beans? Or the Arthurs? I know there's a sassy little aardvark on TV who shares my name and would probably love to be a mascot for a junior high!

So, even though I and my grade nine class wouldn't get the thrill of seeing a new little Arthur cheering everyone on, it would warm my heart to think of him.

It's time to change the mascot. But hey, that's . . . Just One Guy's Opinion.

Hey, Artie!

Nice work on your final article. It's not what I was expecting, but I chuckled at the idea of you being our mascot. That's never BEAN done before!

Thanks again for all your hard work on the newspaper these past three years. I've been constantly amazed by your ability to spin stories in a unique direction. It's like you work in a fabric store, you have so much material!

Good luck next year, Artie. I wish you every success!

Cheers!
Mr. E.

did u talk to camp? did u get a job?

Um, no. I didn't.

didnt talk 2 them or didnt get a job?

Neither. My dad wants to go to Yukon this summer, so I can't work.

what? when did this happen?

He mentioned it a couple of weeks ago. I asked if you could come too! But he said no.

dude this is a total bummer

were not going 2 see each other at all

it wont be the same w/out u

I know. I'm really sorry.

I'm not gone all summer though. We can hang out. Maybe they'll let me stay out there a couple of nights. I could help you.

hopfully. that would be cool

But you're moving back to Calgary for high school, right?

dont think so. hayleys here and the high school has a good football team i want to get on

Oh. It won't be the same without you.

dont cry 2 much. calgary floods pretty easy

have fun at ur grad. ours sucked and was over by 9

Kennedy's in charge of ours, so I bet it's pretty fun.

▶▶ ▶▶ ▶▶

June 21st

Dear RJ,

So. The Grad Dance. I don't know where to start; I guess at the beginning. First, I wore high-tops with my suit, like Ben said that he was going to, and it looked so cool. Both of us had shades too, so we looked like a pair of rock stars when we got there. I could tell that Millie and Joie were impressed. And picking up Joie went all right. Her mom wanted to get a picture of us together, which was weird, because it wasn't like we were going to grad together together. But Joie looked really hot. She even had high heels on. I did not picture her as someone who would wear high heels. She said that she got her dress at a vintage store, so it wasn't even new. It was actually really old, from the 50s! When we got to the dance, Mrs. Ireland made a comment that she had a dress like it for her prom. Can you imagine?! It's hard to even imagine that she wasn't born seventy years old.

When we got to Von's, we were the first ones there, but as soon as Millie and Ben got there, Joie stuck to Millie's side and kind of ignored me. Well, not really. She kept looking at me. Or at least, whenever I looked at her, I think she was already looking at me. Which was weird, but then she would roll her eyes at whatever Von was bragging about, which was funny.

The dance itself wasn't as fun as the stuff beforehand at Von's house. Kennedy and her friends were greeting people at the door, and she looked at me kind of funny when we all came in. The theme was One Night in Paris, and they had decorated the gym with fairy lights and a giant wooden Eiffel Tower. We all had to walk in under the Eiffel Tower so that the photographer could take everyone's picture. The Leg Breaker crew all walked in together, so we took one big group photo. Well, Millie and Ben went back and took one of just the two of them. All the food was French themed, so there was mini-quiches and baguettes and chocolate croissants and cucumbers (I don't know how those are French). Joie joked that everything sounds cooler when you add the word "French" in front of it. French vanilla, French mint, French maid, French fries . . . ha! The idea still makes me laugh.

We danced as a group most of the night, which was fun. Ben's a really good dancer. He said that he was in ballet and tap as a kid, which was funny, because I would never admit that! But he seemed totally cool about it. I don't know how he can be so cool all the time.

At one point, I saw Kennedy and she was standing all by herself, so I went over to say hi and tell her that the grad committee did a good job, but as soon as I got over to her, I just said, "I hope you get good photos for the newspaper," and then I went back to my friends. I realized that I didn't really have much to say to her. I kind of wonder what I ever saw in her in the first place.

So, overall, the night was all right, but I don't think it was really worth all the fuss. My original play would have brought as much joy to people as the wooden Eiffel Tower did. I give it a 7 out of 10.

Yours truly,
Arthur Bean

▸▸ ▸▸ ▸▸

so . . . did u kiss her???

Kiss who?

joey

228

Joie? No. We're not together.

reeeeeaallllyyy . . .

I don't think she likes me like that. We're just friends.

mmmhmmmmm

Do you think she likes me?

no no. im sure she went with u to ur grad cuz she felt sorry for u

Seriously? You think she likes me?

u should go out w her. its way nicer to date some1 who actually likes u

▶▶ ▶▶ ▶▶

June 24th

Dear RJ,

We did the first two plays today at lunch. They went pretty good! Hark said that he thought they were amazing and that we had done a fantastic job of making them look really professional. Von forgot his lines at one part, so he started improvising lines, which made Latha start giggling. I was stage managing, and I was so glad I wasn't onstage with them. It looked really dumb. But once they got through that part, it was pretty good. There weren't a ton of people there, but Kraleigh came (I think she was there more to check on us and make sure that we were "appropriate"), and Ms Whitehead and Mr. Everett were there too. They both promised that they would come to see my play tomorrow. I hope we're ready. I will literally kill Von if he forgets his lines and makes stuff up during my play.

Yours truly,
Arthur Bean

Assignment: How to Survive Junior High

By Arthur Bean

There are few things in life as complicated as junior high. I don't know who thought that junior high was a good idea; at any moment any one of 300 students could burst into any number of things — song, flames, tears, fisticuffs, you name it. The only manual that even comes close to being helpful is *The Hunger Games*. Having lived through thirty months of junior high, I want to take this opportunity to arm you with a few tools that could help you get through.

1. First off, grow several centimetres. The earlier you do this, the better your chances of succeeding. The tallest students are always the coolest. Teachers place them in the back rows,

they get picked to be on sports teams and they are generally considered hotter.

2. Next, don't talk. This is especially true in class when the teacher asks for a volunteer. The only person who likes the volunteer is the teacher. Trust me on this one. The quieter you are, the better the chance that girls will think you're brooding, and they'll probably think you're brooding over them. If they ask if this is true, remember the rule: don't talk. If you actually talk and tell them how you feel, they'll probably ignore you for the rest of junior high.

3. The next thing is that you should be nice to your teachers. Don't do this out in the open, but it's really important. The nicer you are to them, the better your marks will be. But don't, I repeat, don't bring them gifts. You have to be secretly nice to them. You could be that student that they remember forever, and even on their deathbed, they think over their life and say softly, "I wonder if Arthur is still writing . . ." You can give their life true meaning. Plus, another reason you should be nice is because you never know when they might have terrible lives outside of school. Their dog might have diabetes, or maybe they got dumped, or maybe they invested their money badly and now they're teaching to stay out of a homeless shelter. You would have a bad day too if you were teaching to stay out of a homeless shelter. It's our job as students to make sure that teachers have an OK time at work. We need to give back a little.

4. Lastly, I encourage you to break some rules. Not all the rules, and definitely not the big ones, but if you always follow all the rules, you'll have

a really boring life. Plus, you'll have no friends, or your friends will be really boring. It's also a good idea to not get caught breaking the rules, but if you can kind of slip into conversations sometimes that you did break a rule here and there, that will make you cooler.

I could go on, and share other things that I've learned, but one thing that I've learned is to not share everything all the time. That makes you more mysterious, and cooler. I think you need to follow all these rules if you want to make the most of junior high, but if you're anything like me, this should be treated as law.

Arthur,

This may be how you feel about junior high, but this is not the best advice to be passing along to younger students.

I was hoping that you would reveal a reflective side that you haven't demonstrated in your other assignments here, but I'm glad to see that you'll be leaving Terry Fox Jr. High with your sense of humour firmly intact.

Ms Whitehead

Dear Ms Whitehead,

I don't know what you mean by my "reflective side." Do you mean like a mirror? Because every day I look into a mirror, and all I see is a funny guy, trying to share his genius ideas with the world. Don't forget the name <u>Arthur Bean</u>, Ms Whitehead. I'm going to make it big one day, and it might be partly due to you. Maybe I'll thank you in a speech or name a character after you or something when I'm famous. Teachers like that kind of thing, right?

Yours truly,
Arthur Bean

▶▶ ▶▶ ▶▶

June 25th

Dear RJ,

My play was AWESOME!!! People came to see it (WAY more people than came to yesterday's plays). They laughed at all the right places, and the lightsaber fight was amazing. We added a blackout, so it was just the light from the lightsabers and people talking, and it looked awesome. It was so tense! Millie and I did such a good job at it. Ben was hilarious, and Von remembered all his lines, and I looked out in the audience and even Kraleigh was smiling at my jokes. It was such a rush. I've never felt so good before. I really wish my mom could have been there. I know that there were no parents there anyway, but it would have been cool to see her see me onstage. Kennedy came too, which surprised me, since I thought she would never come. She even complimented me on the show afterwards. Well, not really me, but I heard her talking to Latha and Millie and telling them that it was really funny. I'm pretty sure she was telling them loudly enough that I would overhear her.

Anyway, RJ, I'm hooked. From now on, I want to write and star in plays. Hark even pulled me aside and said that my play was some of the best student work he had ever seen and that I should consider putting it in for the fringe festival next year. I didn't know what the fringe festival is, but Hark said that it's a city-wide play festival where you can do anything you want. It sounds awesome. You can even win awards there, and make money, so then if I do that, maybe I won't need to ever get a summer job; I could just do my plays in the summers and make money that way. Hark said that I should come back and visit him at school next year and let him know what I'm up to. I'm sure that I will. After all, who knows what kind of teachers I could have in high school.

Yours truly,
Arthur Bean

▶▶ ▶▶ ▶▶

LAST DAY!!!

Really? We have school tomorrow as well.

ur a sucker. were done today!

Are you coming to Calgary on your way to camp?

ya, just 4 the w-end

Cool, I'll see you Saturday then! We don't leave until July 5th or something.

have fun @ school tomorrow. hayley and i r going to the lake w/ a bunch of friends

Tomorrow's just our grad assembly. It should be pretty good. I just have to think of something clever to write in people's yearbooks . . .

what about have a good summer . . .

from your fave human BEAN

I swear, you want me to get beat up.

HAHAHAHA

▶▶ ▶▶ ▶▶

June 27th

Dear RJ,

School's out! It turns out the grad assembly was really boring, and kind of anti-climactic. We walked across the stage and shook hands with Kraleigh (I almost did a fake-out, but I chickened out at the last minute), then there was a long speech about following your dreams, and they handed out a bunch of awards. I didn't win any, but neither did Von, and he had been talking about how he was going to, so that was awesome. Kennedy won the leadership award she was so intent on winning. She got a fancy watch, which is weird because I don't know anyone other than my dad who still wears a watch. Isn't that what phones are for?

There were lots of parents there as well. I felt bad for them for having to sit through the assembly. Dad came, and took some photos, but I don't know why; we didn't have grad gowns or anything. Everyone just dressed a little bit nicer. Von wore a full suit, which was hilarious because he was the only one. He didn't seem to mind though. I would have hated to be the only one dressed super formally. I went out for pizza and bowling afterwards with the other Leg Breakers (we've decided to keep the name since it's so good). Even though Joie doesn't go to our school, she came. And she sat beside me at the restaurant. It kind of made me nervous. I don't know why that made me feel so nervous, it's not like we're dating.

The restaurant was the best part. I heard a bunch of guys were having a party, but we decided that it would be more fun to not hang around them and to do our own thing. There's always so much drama at their parties, anyway. That's not my style.

It's a bit weird to go into the summer knowing that next year everything will be so different. There are four different junior highs that feed into our high school, like Joie's school and a few others. At least all the Leg Breakers will be there. We're all going to take Drama. And I'll still have you around, RJ. I mean, at least for a bit. I guess Reading Journals are good for something.

Yours truly,
Arthur Bean

YEAR-END REPORT CARD

Arthur showed significant improvement over the year. It was a real delight to read his assignments, and he was able to achieve the three personal goals he set for himself at the beginning of the year. More than that, it has been wonderful to see Arthur mature as a writer and a student over the past three years. I wish him the very best in high school, and I look forward to seeing his first novel in print one day.

Ms Whitehead

Arthur Bean
English 9C — Ms Whitehead
Year-End Summary

Goals for the Year	Complete
Reviewing Personification	80%
Onomatopoeia Comic	85%
Literary Devices Summary	88%
Novel Study	87%
Book Response: Novel	92%
Winter Break Excuses	92%
Book Response: Biography	68%
Superstitions	74%
Design a Set	77%
Macbeth Scenes	95%
Macbeth Review	78%
Book Response: Non-fiction	60%
Extreme Survival!	75%
Personal Reflections: What Is Junior High?	77%

From: Joie Vinh (joievinh@gmail.com)
To: Arthur Bean (arthuraaronbean@gmail.com)
Sent: June 30, 11:22

Yo! Bean!

I read the wolf book you recommended and you're right. It's awesome. I'll have to give it back to you, plus I have a book that, I think, will Blow. Your. Mind. I can hear your brain exploding already. Don't read it in your tent in the Yukon, or else the bears will come to eat your exploded brains, and your poor dad will have to fend off grizzlies that have developed a taste for human flesh. Sigh. Poor Ernie Bean.

Do you think we'll get to hang out before you go? At the risk of sounding all weird and gushy, I'd really like to hang out with just you before you possibly die in the wilds of the Canadian North. But if you don't want to, that's OK. I understand that you may need time to practise your gold-panning skills. All that swirling, and dipping . . . it can be hard work.

Man, I don't know how to end this email. I'm so awkward. This is so awkward. Maybe I should pretend that something terrible is about to happen so that it's not awkward.

Oh! I have to go! There's a giant alligator coming out of the sewer. I think it's trying to eaaaatttttt . . .

Joie

Thank you to Anne Shone, Erin Haggett, Aldo Fierro, Nikole Kritikos, Maral Maclagan and the whole team at Scholastic, with an extra-special thank you to Sandy Bogart Johnston, editor and human extraordinaire — thank you for guiding me through the new waters of writing a trilogy. Also, a loud shout-out to Simon Kwan for amazing illustrations that make me laugh each time I see a new one; my favourite is the one with the fencing podium.

Thank you to Hilary McMahon for being in my corner, and to Tanya Lloyd Kyi, Shannon Ozirny, Kallie George, Lori Sherritt-Fleming, Maryn Quarless and Christy Goerzen for all their advice, support and wisdom.

I'm eternally grateful to be surrounded by love from my family and for all they do for me. Anna, Robert, Diane, Curtiss, Andrew and Chelsey: you mean the world to me, along with the rest of the Matson and Sashaw clans. Yes, Denise. That includes you.

My love goes to Kamila Zloty: the Millie to my Joie, the Betty to my Al. I can't believe we didn't become professional fencers. We were so dedicated!

And, very importantly: Ross Hodgson, Jason Patrick Rothery and Ethan Cole, three fellows who have served as the muses for this book. I'd have never had the idea for this one without you.

About the Author

The first book about Arthur A. Bean, *A Year in the Life of a (Total and Complete) Genius*, began as Stacey Matson's master's thesis at the University of British Columbia. The book went on to win the Chocolate Lily Award, and was short-listed for the Manitoba Young Readers' Choice Award, the Snow Willow Award and the Rocky Mountain Book Award. It was also chosen by the Canadian Children's Book Centre for *Best Books for Kids & Teens*, 2015. The second book in the series, *Scenes from the Epic Life of a Total Genius*, was short-listed for the Manitoba Young Readers' Choice Award and was a starred selection in *Best Books for Kids & Teens*, 2016.

Stacey has an intriguingly varied list of non-writing occupations. She has managed the tour and theatre program on Parliament Hill; created interpretation programs for the Glenbow Museum, Fort Calgary and the Vancouver Aquarium; run a Christmas-tree lot; worked as a forklift operator; and performed as a fairy princess at birthday parties. Stacey was recently selected by the Writers' Trust of Canada as a writer-in-residence at Berton House in Dawson City, Yukon.

Praise for *A Year in the Life of a (Total and Complete) Genius* and *Scenes from the Epic Life of a Total Genius*

"At once funny, outrageous, thoughtful, and informative . . . this is a story with something for everyone, and Arthur's is a voice readers won't soon forget. Give to fans of Susin Nielsen's *Word Nerd*."
—*CM: Canadian Review of Materials*

"[A] splendid debut middle grade novel."
—*The Vancouver Sun*

"An ideal tool to jumpstart a conversation about the subtleties of social interaction and how people communicate, while still being a light and funny read."
—*Quill & Quire*